Other Works

The Cryptid Zoo Series
Cryptid Zoo
Cryptid Island
Cryptid Country
Cryptid Circus

The Death Crawlers Series
Death Crawlers
Deep in the Jungle
The Next World
Battleground Earth

Standalone Titles
Salurid
Creatures

IN CASE OF CARNAGE

IN CASE OF CARNAGE

Gerry Griffiths

Epic Publishing
Pittsburgh

First Printing: 2020

ISBN 978-1-7346486-0-7

Epic Publishing
www.epic-publishing.com

Special discounts are available on quantity purchases. For details, contact the publisher by email at the following address:

Epic Publishing
370 Castle Shannon Blvd., #10366
Pittsburgh, PA 15234

For Lori Michelle

Thank you for opening the door and showing the way.

1

CASE NUMBER: 18-01-236

Clare Carver placed her bulky forensic kit by the body, avoiding the pool of blood inches away from Detective Bill Hendrix's patent leather shoes. He observed her methodical process, jotting down specifics in his notepad.

The victim was a teenage girl, possible runaway. Skin smooth as Philadelphia cream cheese. Black Hot Topic T-shirt with a crudely cut hole haloing a green barbell belly button ring. Designer blue jeans fashionably snipped away at the knees. Red Keds high-tops without shoelaces. Green spiked hair in the rust-colored blood on the cement floor.

Bill crouched to inspect the weepy quarter-inch hole in her forehead, the gold shield on his belt digging into his gut. He noticed puncture marks on the girl's neck, just under her right ear.

"Are those incisor wounds on her throat?"

Clare leaned forward for a closer look. "Possibly."

"Too clean for an animal bite."

"What are you suggesting?"

"I'd say it's the work of a vampire."

Clare gave him an incredulous look before bursting into laughter.

"Better not let Hank hear you say that." Clare glanced at Bill's gun. "Is that a snub-nosed thirty-eight?"

"Smith and Wesson. Same as Hank carries. Why?"

"They still make those? When are you guys going to get with the latest department issue?"

"What, those plastic guns? No thanks." Bill shook his head, noting Clare's firearm strapped to her side.

Clare pulled her handgun with slick precision. "You're looking at a Glock 29 ten-millimeter with a ten-round clip, polymer frame, and non-corrosive coating, so it won't rust like those pea-shooters you two call guns," she bragged before holstering her weapon. "Standard issue, per the captain."

"Hey, a *lot* of famous detectives carried thirty-eights. *Dragnet's* Sergeant Joe Friday, Jim Rockford in *The Rockford Files*."

"Bill, those guys weren't even real cops. Please don't tell me you're packing those three-eighty automatics around your ankles."

"They're great little backup guns."

"Next you're going to tell me you use speedloaders." She laughed, patting the two ten-round clips on her belt next to the tactical folding knife in a Velcro sheath beside her holstered high-tech semi-automatic.

Bill was about to reach into his jacket pocket when a mall security guard came into the room looking like he had just left his mother's funeral.

"What are you two squabbling about?" Detective Hank Jenkins entered the storeroom right behind the despondent security guard. Hank slipped the man's firearm in an evidence bag.

"Where's Silverman?" Bill asked. Normal protocol required that the first uniformed officer on the crime scene be present to answer questions during the primary investigation.

"Other side of the mall. Checking surveillance."

"Bill thinks the girl was bitten by a vampire." Clare pointed at the dead girl's neck.

"Jeez, Bill. Can't you be serious for one minute?"

The disgruntled mall guard glanced at the dead girl, then stared down at his boots. "I can't believe it. I take this lousy job to subsidize my pissant retirement, and look what happens."

"Bill, this is Ralph Talbert," Hank said.

Bill nodded at the security guard.

Hank said to Ralph, "Tell my partner what you told me."

Ralph cleared his throat. "The last few days there have been a number of break-ins in the mall."

Bill asked, "Why didn't the mall manager report them?"

"Maybe he was in on it. I don't know."

"Go on."

"They cut the padlocks on the metal gates, crawl under and jimmy the entry doors. So far, they've broken into about eight different stores."

Bill asked, "What are they after?"

"Well, it's weird. This mall's got tons of electronics stores, stuff you could make good money selling at the flea market. These guys? They take clothes. They've even raided the kitchens in the food court."

"How are they getting into the mall if the outside doors are locked?"

"Personally, I think it's an employee who has access to a master key." Ralph glanced over at the dead girl. "I swear, one of them was pointing a gun at me."

Hank asked, "What do you mean, 'one of them'?"

"There were two."

Hank gave Ralph a hard stare.

Ralph shrugged. "Jesus, I thought I told you."

A loud crash came from the main floor of the sporting goods store.

"What was that?" Bill snatched his gun out of the shoulder rig.

Hank stuffed Ralph's gun into the side pocket of his coat. He drew his .38 snub-nosed out of the holster clipped to his belt.

Clare threw back the slide on her Glock.

Hank and Bill went first. Clare stepped out next with Ralph trailing behind her.

The sporting goods showroom was cast in shadows. A majority of the overhead fluorescent panels were turned off to conserve energy.

Hank spotted movement to his right. He signaled Bill and Clare.

A scrawny teenager stood in front of a smashed display case, shoving small boxes into a rucksack.

"Let's see those hands!" Bill barked. "This is the—"

IN CASE OF CARNAGE

The kid swiveled around with a shotgun. The muzzle flash lit up as the boom thundered in the room. Bill shoved Clare to the floor and dove on top of her. Pumping another cartridge into the chamber, the gunman swung the barrel and blasted again. A rack of sleeping bags exploded in a goose down blizzard.

Hank fired a quick shot, striking the kid in the shoulder. The impact sent him toppling into the display case.

Bill got up. Clare sprang to her feet.

"I only winged him," Hank cautioned.

The teenage boy lay on the floor amid ammunition boxes covered with glass shards. Hank kicked the shotgun out of the kid's reach. Bill and Clare kept their guns trained on the suspect.

"Please don't kill me," the kid begged.

"You're lucky we didn't." Bill grabbed the shotgun off the floor.

"Wait a minute. You're not them."

"Who did you *think* we were?"

"Aw man, you're the cops!"

"Hey, where's Ralph?" Hank turned, scouting the store for the security guard.

"Over there." Clare pointed.

Ralph was dead on the floor, sprawled under the glow of a ceiling light. His face was a bloody pulp, riddled with buckshot, looking like the inside of a pomegranate.

Hank stared at the wounded teenager. "You screwed up big time, son."

Bill bent down to scrutinize the boy. "He's got the same bite marks on his neck as the girl."

A red blossom bloomed on the boy's shirt. The bullet

had struck the right deltoid a couple of inches away from the shoulder.

Clare holstered her Glock. "I need to stop the bleeding." She took a pair of blue gloves out of her pants pocket. She stretched the elastic before slipping them on. "Hand me one of those shirts for a compress."

Bill grabbed a shirt off a rack. Clare wadded it up and placed it over the wound. She took the boy's left hand and pressed it palm-side down on the compress. "What's your name?"

"Peter."

"Okay, Peter. Keep applying pressure."

Clare glanced down at the boy's right arm. "Guys, look at this."

Two puncture marks on the forearm, too large for needle tracks.

"Jesus, Peter," Clare said, "Who did this to you?"

"The vampires."

Hank shook his head. "Kid, you're in enough trouble. What are you even doing in here?"

"We thought it would be cool to hide out in the mall after it closed."

"When was that?"

"I don't know. A week ago?"

Hank saw the surprised looks on Bill and Clare's faces. "Weren't you afraid of getting caught?"

"We'd smoked a bunch of weed."

"So who's your girlfriend?"

"Sissy."

"Tell us about the bite marks."

Peter must have pressed too hard on his wound

because he crinkled up his face. "They feed on us. I'm a donor. Sissy's a blood doll. They take turns, pass us around like a bottle of Jim Beam."

"So you and Sissy broke into those stores?"

"Yes, they made us."

Hank frowned. "What do you mean, 'made you'? Sounds to me like you could have escaped any time you wanted."

"They have my sister. They're holding her hostage. If we don't do what they want, they'll kill her."

"What's your sister's name?"

"Peg. We needed the gun to rescue her."

"How many of these . . ." Hank paused, rolling his eyes at Bill, "*Vampires* would you say there are?"

"Four. I'm telling you, they're crazy." Peter's eyes widened. "These guys are stronger than shit!" He raised his head off the floor to gaze around. "Hey, where's Sissy?"

Bill broke the news. "Your girlfriend is dead. The guard you killed shot her."

Peter scrunched his eyes shut, tears leaking down his cheeks.

Hank asked, "Where are they keeping your sister?"

"Under the mall."

"How do we find her?"

"Follow the corridor at the food court to the restrooms. The 'Employees Only' door to the right of the men's room is unlocked. Take the stairs down to the basement. There's a huge tunnel the delivery trucks use. Go right until you see a big 'W2' stenciled on the wall to your left with a black door. Their hideout is in there."

Bill scowled. "You know, we have a problem."

Hank let out a sigh. "And what is that?"

"They're vampires."

"This is a bunch of bull."

"You know bullets won't kill them."

"My Glock will," Clare chimed in.

"That might slow them down a bit"—Bill raised his eyebrows—"until the lead pops out of their bodies. There're only four ways you can kill a vampire." He counted them off on his fingers. "Drive a stake through their heart, cut off their head, expose them to sunlight, or set them on fire."

"I can't believe I'm standing here listening to this nonsense," Hank said. "Let's go find these jokers."

Clare used her cell phone to call the security office. She told Officer Silverman to get back to the sporting goods store, on the double to watch Peter. She then called dispatch to summon an ambulance and notify the captain of their situation. Hank handcuffed Peter's right hand to a pole next to the display case.

"Don't move. Someone will be here shortly." Clare stripped off her gloves.

They hustled out of the sporting goods store and dashed down the wide corridor that separated the specialty shops. Officer Silverman was already jogging in their direction and gave them a wave.

After reaching the food court, they headed for the restrooms. Hank spotted the door: Employees Only. It was unlocked, so he pushed it open. Cement stairs stretched down into the tenebrous gloom of the underground tunnels. He started down, Bill a step behind, Clare taking up the rear.

Halfway down, Hank heard a crack. He glanced over his shoulder. "What was that?"

Bill held up what looked like a stick.

"Is that an arrow?"

"Yeah, I broke off the metal tip."

"Why?"

"The shaft has to be made solely of wood when driven through a vampire's heart."

Hank looked at what Bill had in his other hand. "You took a crossbow?"

"Yeah, I grabbed it on our way out of the store, along with some arrows." Bill pulled another arrow out of the short quiver that was sticking out of the side pocket of his jacket. He pressed the end against the concrete wall, snapping the tip off.

"Jesus, I don't believe you!" Hank continued down.

Clare tapped Bill on the shoulder. "Jeez, Bill. You're really serious about this."

"Clare, they're vampires."

"You know, it might not hurt to have a little chat with the departmental shrink."

"Why? 'Cause you're dating him?"

"No, I'm not!"

"Not what *I* heard."

"Okay, we went out *once*, but—"

Hank barked from the bottom of the stairs, "Will you two keep it down!"

Clare and Bill rushed down the steps and joined Hank. They stood in the middle of a large tunnel with loading docks stretching in both directions, tapering into the darkness.

"The only way to gain access from the outside is through one of those entrances, which are controlled by the guard in the security office." Hank pointed to an automatic roll-up door.

The tunnel was nearly twenty feet high—wide enough for two big rig trailers to squeeze past each other going in opposite directions. A network of yellow globe lights, various-sized plumbing pipes, and conduits of electrical wiring ran along the ceiling. The nearest loading dock had the store's name stenciled on the side of the concrete ramp.

Farther on they found the black door next to the large "W2" painted on the wall. Hank stood on one side of the door, one hand on the handle. Bill and Clare steeled themselves against the wall.

Hank flung open the door. They stormed in—Hank sweeping left, Clare taking the right, and Bill up the middle—panning their guns about the large room. It looked like a den for the homeless. Filthy sleeping bags were strewn across the floor. Black garbage bags bulged with stolen merchandise. Empty food containers were tossed in a corner. Trash was scattered everywhere. The stale, putrid air reeked of body odor and filthy clothes.

The room was deserted.

"Maybe they heard the gunshots." Bill kicked a shoebox across the floor.

"I heard something!" Clare bolted out of the room. The two detectives charged out after her.

"There they are!" Clare pointed to two figures racing down the tunnel.

A scream came from the opposite direction.

IN CASE OF CARNAGE

"Damn, they split up," Hank said. "Bill, Clare, go that way. I'll follow these two."

* * *

They were faster than a pair of doped-up track runners. The way they ran reminded Hank of apes loping in the jungle. The sounds of their feet slapping the pavement let him know they were barefoot. Probably didn't have time to put on shoes. He wondered if they were armed.

His legs were already starting to burn. He needed to get back to his routine morning jogs, devote fewer hours behind the desk.

Hank slowed as he reached a bend in the tunnel. If they were smart, they would wait in ambush, attack when he came running blindly around the corner.

He stopped for a second to listen. He could hear air flowing through the ducts above his head, liquid surging down the pipes. Somewhere behind the walls, machines hummed, busy at work.

Hank slid along the concrete wall, edging around the bend. He found himself standing below the loading dock with the sporting goods store logo.

A forklift was parked on one side of the huge platform. Empty pallets were stacked high against a wall near a control panel for a giant gray compactor—the kind for flattening cardboard boxes. The twin doors remained open on the hopper, like crushing jaws waiting for a victim.

Half a dozen pallets stood in front of the closed door of the receiving area with merchandise covered in shrink-wrap. Hank pointed his .38, climbing the short flight of concrete steps leading to the platform. He crept past the forklift to the first pallet.

He could see the labels through the shrink-wrap: boxed camping stoves and cases of kerosene. He squeezed between two more pallets stacked high with boxes. It was like being wedged inside a narrow passage. A pallet skidded toward Hank, threatening to crush him against the pallet directly behind him.

He was shocked to see the forklift parked, unmanned, on the other side of the loading dock. Hank escaped from between the pallets before they slammed together.

A hulking figure stood only five feet away.

Hank closed his eyes briefly, thinking he was seeing things. When he reopened them, it was still standing there.

Maybe Bill was right. Maybe they *did* exist.

The only vampire Hank had ever seen was on the cover of a DVD case Bill had shown him to persuade him to take the movie home to watch. The vampire? Bela Lugosi, creepy with his sinister stare and lecherous grin, but still resembling a man.

Not *this* vampire.

Two short, stubby horns jutted from its forehead, its head smooth and hairless. Its face and scalp were inked with swirling, weird symbols and stars. Its eyebrows, both sides of its nose, lips, and even its chin, were pierced with rings and metal studs. Its earlobes were grotesquely enlarged with black disks. Its eyes were shaded with mascara, and its pupils were eerie, thin slits against green serpentine irises.

It stood about five-ten, wearing a tight-fitting black

IN CASE OF CARNAGE

T-shirt and dark jeans. Its bulging muscles were a road-map of ropy veins ready to burst, rippling like those of a bodybuilder on steroids.

The vampire opened its mouth, giving Hank a preview of things to come.

Hank couldn't believe the size of its fangs. Every tooth had been filed to a tiny point, and its tongue was forked like a serpent's.

"Don't move! You're under arrest!" Hank reached under his jacket for his handcuffs when the vampire charged.

Hank fired two quick rounds, nailing the bloodsucker in the chest.

The vampire didn't even flinch. It looked down at the bullet holes in its T-shirt. It dabbed some blood with its finger, ran the tip over its tongue.

Hank aimed for the thing's ugly head and pulled the trigger.

The bullet grazed the side of the vampire's skull, clipping off a horn. Blood gushed out and down its face. The vampire ran across the loading dock, one hand clamped on its head.

"Stop!" Hank shouted.

The vampire vaulted onto the rim of the compactor's hopper. It was about to jump up onto the main housing when Hank fired again.

The bullet struck the vampire in the leg, causing it to tumble into the hopper.

Hank ran over. "Give it up!" He kept his gun trained on the creature. He warily approached until he was within a foot.

The vampire lunged, its long, sharp nails piercing Hank's jacket. One powerful yank slammed him up against the steel wall of the hopper.

The vampire glared, flicking its tongue.

Hank reached back with one hand, his fingers fumbling blindly on the control panel. He punched the red button.

The hopper motor rumbled, then roared. The twin doors began their slow descent to crush the contents of the bin.

Instead of trying to escape the hopper, the vampire started to drag Hank over the rim.

Hank hooked the toe of his shoe under a lip of metal near the floor, anchoring himself. He grabbed the metal face to push back. The vampire refused to budge.

Hank shot the vampire's hand that was clutching his jacket. The bullet ripped through the palm, blowing out a bloody chunk from the back of its hand. Its grip relaxed, enabling Hank to pull free—just as the heavy doors came down on the fiend's neck. The pistons pushed the doors deep inside the hopper like a guillotine, decapitating the vampire.

Hank hit the red button, switching off the machine.

A hand gripped Hank's shoulder, hoisted him in the air, and threw him fifteen feet across the loading dock. The security guard's gun fell out of his pocket. His service revolver clattered across the concrete loading dock.

Another vampire skulked from behind the pallets, its face the spitting image of the one dead in the hopper.

***

IN CASE OF CARNAGE

Bill and Clare were on the far side of the underground passage when they heard the first shots.

"Do you think Hank's okay?" Clare slowed down to glance back.

"Hank can take care of himself."

They edged around a bend in the tunnel.

"Where'd they go?" Clare aimed her Glock, ready for anything.

They stood in the middle of the thoroughfare between two loading docks.

Bill craned his neck to look up. "Careful, they could be—"

A woman screamed on the loading dock to their right.

"Cover me." Bill dashed up the concrete steps.

When he reached the top, a muscular creep with facial tattoos—*Christ, are those horns?*—and black clothing held a teenage girl hostage.

"Let the girl go!" Bill loaded an arrow into the crossbow. "Are you Peg?"

The girl hitched a breath, unable to speak. The vampire laughed when it saw Bill's weapon. With one hand, it wrapped its fingers around Peg's neck and raised her off her feet.

Bill leveled the crossbow. The creature glared, revealing razor-point fangs, and laughed. Bill took his shot. The vampire bellowed when the arrow buried itself into its right shin. It dropped the girl. Peg scampered toward Bill.

He cocked back the bowstring and slipped another arrow into the crossbow. He waited for Peg to get out of his line of fire, then pulled the trigger. The arrow sailed to the right of the vampire.

The vampire flew at Bill. It grabbed the detective,

baring its fangs. It bit through his jacket clear down to the flesh of his shoulder.

"Son of a—" Bill reached down, jiggled the arrow in the vampire's shin. The vampire howled, shoving Bill back. Bill snatched another arrow from the quiver in his pocket. He drove the jagged tip into the vampire's heart.

The vampire gasped, flailing back its arms. It landed on the hard cement with a heavy thud.

Bill looked at the trembling teenager. "You're safe now." He staggered over to the edge of the loading dock. "Clare! I've got the girl!"

But Clare was gone.

* * *

The vampire stood beside a pallet of outdoor equipment. Hank drew the .380 automatic from his ankle holster. The vampire took one look at the puny gun and laughed. Hank fired three shots anyway.

None of them hit the vampire. Instead, the bullets struck the bottom boxes on the pallet next to the vampire. Bubbling liquid leaked onto the cement dock.

The vampire stared down at its bare feet in the expanding puddle. It took a deep whiff, eyes wide with alarm.

Hank fired a single shot. The bullet ricocheted off the concrete, the spark igniting the fumes. Flames whooshed up all around the vampire before it could even think to run. The fire swept up its pant legs, consuming its body in a spiraling torch.

Hank rolled across the cement and dropped over the

edge of the loading dock.

The shipment of kerosene camping fuel exploded off the pallet.

***

Clare wakened, slumped over the vampire's shoulder. It was jogging down the tunnel, carrying her as if she weighed no more than a five-pound sack of potatoes.

She could see a radiant glow further down the tunnel.

Blood ran down her sleeve. Her neck stung. *Oh, God, I've been bitten by a vampire!*

She'd lost her Glock, had dropped it when the creature clobbered her head. She reached around to her gun belt. She drew her combat knife, unfolded the blade.

The vampire slowed its pace, turning its head. Clare got her first glimpse of its face. With horns, it looked like the devil incarnate, its face disfigured with ink and metal studs. The abomination sneered, displaying its filed teeth. A serpent tongue flicked out of its mouth.

Clare stabbed the vampire in the side. She kept jabbing it until it finally released her legs. She slipped off its shoulder and landed on her feet.

The vampire stopped, glaring at her.

Clare thrust the blade into its neck.

A wail gurgled from between its thin lips. The creature stumbled off toward a nearby ramp.

Clare spotted a green traffic light suspended on the ceiling. A massive rollup door began to rise. Blinding light poured into the tunnel entrance. Clare shielded her eyes with her hand.

The vampire screamed.

Clare recalled Bill's words. Direct sunlight could kill a vampire. But this couldn't be sunlight; it was hours before daybreak.

She strained to see in the blinding glare of the head-lamps as the fire engine barreled down the ramp.

The bumper smacked the vampire, throwing it under the truck. A wide tread tire drove over the vampire's body, flattening its head.

***

Bill stared at the bland food on his lunch tray. He was bare-chested, as he had a large bandage covering his right shoulder.

He looked up as Hank and Clare entered his hospital room. Clare brought a bouquet of flowers. She placed the vase on the windowsill.

"How're you feeling, buddy?" Hank leaned against the handrail of the bed.

"Lousy. I got bit."

"So did I." Clare showed him the dressing on her neck.

"What happens now?"

"Hank has agreed to put us out of our misery the moment we turn."

Hank nodded and gave his partner a sheepish grin.

"Not funny, Clare."

"Jeez, lighten up, Bill," Clare said. "They weren't vampires, you idiot."

"Then what were they?"

"Vampire wannabes," she answered. "They're called

sanguinarians—blood drinkers. Only *these* guys went to the extreme. The weird tattoos, getting their tongues forked, wearing creepy contact lenses. Those horns on their foreheads were actually titanium implants."

"Why were they so damn strong?"

"Their blood work showed high concentrations of bath salts, some hallucinogens, other weird steroid derivatives," Clare said. "Don't worry. None of them tested positive for HIV. They were so high, they actually believed they were vampires."

"They sure fooled me."

"Yeah, Bill," Hank agreed. "They sure did."

Hank and Clare pulled chairs up to the bedside. The afternoon sun shone through the window. They basked in the warm room, their sole amusement watching Bill pick at his food.

Hank had to admit, even *he* had been fooled by those sanguinarians. Bill and his crazy vampire theories. When would he learn that supernatural stuff was nothing but a bunch of mumbo jumbo and give it a break?

2
CASE NUMBER: 18-01-237

"So what's the occasion? It's not my birthday." Jackie stared over Hank's shoulder, watching their waiter leave after taking their drink orders for pomegranate margaritas. "Can't be our anniversary."

"I didn't forget. You know how busy I am at work." Jackie opened her menu.

"Tell me you're not still mad." Hank gazed lovingly at his wife. She looked especially gorgeous: her blonde hair swept back to show off the pearl earrings her mother had given her, the gentle slope of her delicate neck, which he liked to nuzzle. She was even wearing The Green Dress, which she only wore for fancy dinners.

"Haven't decided yet."

"Have I told you how beautiful you look tonight?"

"Do I detect a lame attempt to get back in my good graces?"

"How am I doing so far?"

"You could step it up a bit."

"I got you something." Hank dipped into the pocket of his suit jacket and took out a small black velvet box. He placed the gift next to Jackie's place setting on the table. "Open it."

Before Jackie could comply, someone at the front of the restaurant yelled something in Spanish.

Hank and Jackie turned.

A disheveled Hispanic man grappled with a waiter, who tried to drag him outside.

"Hank, what's going on?"

"I don't know."

The man looked like a migrant farm worker, his shirt and trousers soiled with dirt. He broke free from the waiter and bolted into the dining area. Many of the customers looked up from their meals in alarm. One woman screamed.

Pandemonium quickly ensued as the man continued to shout in Spanish. He crashed into a table, knocking an elderly man out of his chair. Diners watched nervously as the intruder shambled between the tables.

The crazed man staggered toward Hank and Jackie's table.

"*Por favor, tienes que ayudarme!*" the man pleaded.

Hank pushed away from the table. He raised his hand for the man to halt. "Yes, I'll help you but first you must—"

The man's head exploded.

Wet slop blew into Hank's face, splattering his suit. He wiped the muck from his eyes. Bloody bone fragments littered the white linen tablecloth. Gore covered the nearest walls. Men and women were screaming.

What remained of the Hispanic man's body slumped on the floor. Shredded pieces of his head, shoulders, and arms plastered the restaurant. Arterial spray from the gaping wound soaked the carpet.

A man with a large, jagged piece of projectile bone wedged into his face moaned on the floor. A woman slouched at her table, a bloody hand cupped over her right eye.

Hank examined his ruined suit. He touched the lapel with his forefinger. The blood felt gritty when he rubbed his finger and thumb together.

He glanced over at Jackie. Her hair was drenched, covered in slop. Red globs speckled her face. He knew the cleaners would never be able to salvage the Green Dress.

Jackie unfolded her cloth napkin. She began to clean her face.

Hank grabbed his own napkin. He wiped away the blood and stuffed the small box intended for Jackie into his pocket.

"My God, Hank! What just happened?"

"I don't know." Surely, he would have heard a shotgun blast. What *else* could it have been? Hank drew his revolver, scanning the room for the shooter. Terrified people scrambled for the nearest exit. There was too much noise for Hank to get anyone's attention.

Hank holstered his gun. He helped Jackie up. "Are you hurt?"

"No, I'm fine. Guess I won't be wearing *this* dress again."

"Of all nights, it had to be tonight."

Hank's cell phone rang. "Detective Jenkins," he answered, then paused to listen. "I'll be there as soon as I can." He closed his phone and stuffed it back into his pocket.

"Who was that?" Jackie had managed to remove most of the blood from her face.

"That was Bill. They found some bodies in a warehouse."

"Oh my God. Where?"

"A couple blocks down the street."

***

Hank waited for the uniformed cops to arrive to cordon off the restaurant. He passed on what information he knew to the officer in charge and explained he was needed at another crime scene. Before excusing himself, he gave Jackie a quick kiss and arranged for a patrol car to take her home.

Hank exited the restaurant.

More squad cars and emergency vehicles arrived. Emergency lights flashed further down the street. People stared as he passed them on the sidewalk. His clothes looked as if they'd been processed through a meat grinder. He ignored the gawking. *Hey, when was the last time someone exploded all over you?*

Officer Silverman slouched at the warehouse entrance. When he noticed Hank, his hand twitched on the grip of his sidearm. "Stop right there!"

Hank opened his jacket, displaying the gold shield that was clipped to his belt.

"Sorry, sir. I didn't recognize you. You should see yourself. You look like a zombie."

Hank was in no mood for idle chitchat, especially of the undead sort. "Well, I'm not." He kept on walking and entered the building.

Hank crossed the warehouse floor, its expanse the size of a high school gym. Clare worked the scene in a makeshift laboratory. Fluorescent lights illuminated the sophisticated-looking equipment that was arranged on four long tables. Two high-powered microscopes were on one end of a workbench. Empty wooden shipping crates were stacked against a wall.

"Something tells me this isn't a meth lab."

"And you would be right." Clare didn't bother to look up as she studied something on the floor. "This setup is more for wafer fabrication."

"Like microchips?"

"Right again."

Clare scooped something up in a clear plastic bag. She glanced up at Hank. "I thought you were going out to a nice dinner. What happened? You and Jackie get into a food fight?"

"Where's Bill?"

"In there." Clare pointed at an opened doorway. "I have to warn you. It's pretty bad."

Hank stepped into a dark hallway with a series of doors on each side.

"Bill, you in here?"

"First door on the left. Watch where you step."

IN CASE OF CARNAGE

Hank saw light flickering inside the room. He stood at the threshold and peeked in.

"What do you think?" Bill shined the beam of his flashlight on the blood-stained walls. "An execution room?"

Hank took his small Maglite out of his jacket pocket and shined the flashlight on the ceiling. It looked like the artwork of Sydney Pollack—as if whole cans of red and brown paint had been hurled against the walls and ceiling. "How does blood get all the way up there?"

"Twin barrels under the chin might do it."

"This looks like a torture chamber."

"You might be right. Come see what's in the next room."

This time, there was a decapitated body on the floor—no head anywhere. The upper torso had been savagely hacked, as if someone had shoved it into the mincing blades of a wood chipper.

"There are more in the other rooms just like this one. Looks like they were being kept in holding cells. The doors were locked from the outside." Bill shined his flashlight on Hank. "You look like Carrie after she got dowsed with the bucket of blood."

"Carrie who?"

"You know, *Carrie*, the movie with Sissy Spacek."

Hank was drawing a blank.

"Stephen King?"

Hank shook his head. "It's from the guy who interrupted our dinner."

"Interesting. We got a call that some weirdo was seen leaving this warehouse, yelling his fool head off. Think he's the same guy?"

"If he is, he blew up all over the restaurant."

"Like a suicide bomber?"

"No, I don't think so. Let's see if Clare's found anything. By the way, how's the shoulder?"

"Got my stitches out. Still itches like crazy. Dumb vampire wannabes."

The detectives returned to the laboratory. Clare was sealing an evidence bag. She placed the see-through plastic on a table with the rest of the collected evidence.

"I don't believe these are the beginnings of a start-up company." Clare leaned back against the edge of the table. "Not operating in a warehouse like *this*. For one, wafer fabrication is always done in a clean environment to guard against contaminants. This is something entirely different."

"I'll bet it's somehow linked with human trafficking," Bill said. "Would explain the bodies."

Hank looked over at the table. "So, what have you bagged?"

"Some nine-millimeter cartridges. We'll know more about their origin when I catalog them at the lab. The packing slips on those shipping crates should give us a lead as to who placed the orders and where this equipment came from. We've got hair, chewed gum, cigarette butts, a slaughterhouse full of blood for DNA samples, though I doubt we'll get a match. The medical examiner will have more after the bodies are examined."

Hank glanced over at another table. "Wait a minute—I thought this wasn't a drug operation." He walked over to a stack of clear bags containing a white substance. "Each one of these must be a kilo, easy."

"Try some," Clare said.

"What? Are you crazy?"

"Go ahead."

Hank dabbed the sample of granules that had been poured directly on the table with the tip of his finger. He put his finger up to his mouth, took a lick. He spat it out. "It's sand!"

"Weird, huh?"

"I'll say."

"Come, take a look." Clare stepped over to the next table. "See this dust outline? A piece of equipment was here."

"Anything else?" Hank asked.

"Found this." Clare held up a bag containing a single microchip.

"I wonder what—"

Gunshots erupted outside, followed by a loud peal of screeching tires.

Hank and Bill rushed from the warehouse to discover Officer Silverman kneeling on the sidewalk.

Hank helped him up. "Who shot at you?"

"Not sure. They were in a black Expedition. The windows were tinted. I think it was an Uzi."

Hank looked at Bill. "Drug cartel?"

"That smuggles sand? I doubt it."

***

The next morning, Hank drove their Ford Crown Victoria through a middle-class suburban neighborhood of aging two-story homes, each with a cracked driveway that ran up the property line to a single-car garage tucked in the rear of the backyard.

Bill noted the street numbers on the curb from the passenger window. "Couple more blocks. This Patrick Manning could have covered his tracks better."

"Maybe he left those packing slips on purpose."

Bill studied the report on his lap. "He used to work for a big microchip manufacturer. There was some dispute over patent rights, so he left the company six months ago."

"What was he working on?"

"Doesn't say."

Hank paused at a stop sign. He checked both ways before proceeding down the lane, which was shaded by old elms. "Clare showed the microchip she found to one of her techs, who used to be an electronic engineer."

"That might be a lead."

Hank shook his head. "He'd never seen anything like it before, though he was certain the chip had enormous memory capacity."

"Like what? A super chip for storing data?"

"Some new age technology."

"This is it." Bill pointed to a house with a small patch of brown lawn in the front.

Hank pulled up to the curb. He shut off the engine.

They got out of the patrol car. As they were heading toward the steps to the front porch, Bill suddenly stopped Hank. The detectives stared up the side driveway. A black SUV was parked in front of the single-car garage.

"Could be our Expedition," Bill said.

"Let's go pay them a visit."

IN CASE OF CARNAGE

The detectives drew their weapons. They scurried up the driveway, staying close to the side of the house, ducking each time they came to a window. Edging around the corner, they came to a set of wooden steps leading to the back door.

Hank crept up. He peered through the smudged window.

Two men in plaid shirts sat at the kitchen table, which was cluttered with empty bottles. They were drinking beer, joking in Spanish.

Hank banged the door open. Bill stormed in behind him.

The one with the raven-black ponytail grabbed his Uzi off the table.

Hank shot him two times.

As he flipped backwards in his chair, the man's finger tugged on the trigger. The machine gun sprayed the header above the back door, squiggling up the wall and onto the ceiling.

The other man swung a sawed-off shotgun out from under the table.

Bill nailed him with a slug to the head before he could release a shot.

The man toppled from his chair onto the linoleum floor.

The detectives stood over the bodies.

The kitchen clock on the wall kept ticking, its plastic face cracked from a bullet.

Another sound seemed to be coming from the cellar.

Hank looked at the door leading downstairs. "Man, I *hate* basements!"

"Don't worry. I got your back."

"Gee, thanks."

Hank pushed the door open. He stared down into the gloom for a moment before slowly descending the flight of stairs. Bill followed two steps behind.

Coming off the bottom step, Hank located a light switch on the wall. He flicked it on, illuminating the dank space.

The floor layout looked similar to the equipment table setup at the warehouse.

A man and a woman sat back-to-back, tied together in their chairs. The man wore a white lab coat, the woman a drab dress. Her brown eyes widened with fright, like a deer staring down the headlights of an oncoming car.

Hank stepped in front of the man. "Is there anyone else in the house besides those two upstairs?"

"No, I don't *think* so. Are you the police?"

"That's right."

"Thank God! Can you please untie us?"

"Not until you answer some questions. Are you Patrick Manning?"

"Yes."

"The woman?"

"I believe her name is Anita."

"Mind explaining what you do down here?" Hank waved his hand about the room.

"It's a special project I've been developing for years. Somehow, the cartel got wind of my research. For the past three months, they've been forcing me to devise a new method to smuggle in their drugs. If you'll untie me, I'll show you."

"All right. Keep your hands where we can see them," Hank said.

"I will."

Bill holstered his gun. He reached between the captives and untied the knots. Afraid that she might bolt up the stairs, he motioned for the woman to remain in her chair.

Manning rubbed his wrists. He stood, shook out his legs. Then he went to a nearby table and picked up a device resembling a toy laser gun.

"Hold it!" Hank pointed his revolver at Manning.

"It's not a weapon. It's an injector. They wanted me to inject Anita. Thank God you showed up when you did."

"Inject her with what?" Hank asked.

"This." Manning held up a tiny microchip. He loaded it into the injector, then walked over to the frightened woman. He positioned the end of the injector beneath Anita's collarbone. "Once I press the button, a stream of high-pressure air shoots the chip into her flesh."

"Okay, put it down." Hank kept his gun trained on the scientist.

"I was merely illustrating." Manning returned the injector to the table.

"I still don't follow," Hank said.

"It's all part of my invention." Manning rested his arm on a metallic box. He beamed as though he were about to accept a Nobel Prize for scientific achievement.

"A microwave oven?" Hank couldn't help but laugh.

"Far from it. Allow me to—"

Anita bolted from the chair. She rushed over to a dark

corner of the room and got down on the floor, cowering like a small child afraid of the Boogeyman.

"What did you do to this poor woman?" Hank snapped.

"Believe me, I never wanted to hurt anyone."

"You mean those bodies we found at the warehouse?" Bill interceded. "So what's with the microwave oven?"

"It's actually a converter. I've always been intrigued by the concept of mass conversion. I've developed a way to store physical mass on a microchip, much as data is stored on a computer chip. Allow me to demonstrate."

Hank motioned with his gun. "Don't try anything funny."

Manning opened a cabinet and took out a clear plastic bag filled with white sand, similar to the bags at the warehouse. He swung open the door on the converter, placed the bag inside, and closed the door. Then he grabbed a microchip from a tray and inserted it into a slot on the side of the machine. He took a few seconds to type in a start sequence on a programming panel, then pushed a button.

A steady thrum sounded inside the machine. A bright light flashed behind the glass. The humming stopped.

Manning opened the door on the converter.

The bag was gone.

Hank peeked into the machine. "Where the hell did it go?"

"Right here." Manning plucked the microchip from the slot. "The bag you saw me put inside the converter has now been transferred onto this tiny chip."

"You've discovered a way to miniaturize material onto a microchip?" Hank looked at Bill, who stared by slack-jawed.

"That is correct."

"Talk about wild." Bill kept shaking his head in disbelief.

"So why the bags of sand?" Hank asked.

"They didn't want to waste the actual product," Manning said. "There's a time delay problem with the chip. Every time I injected someone, the matter converted onto the chips expanded unexpectedly, usually within the hour, causing the subject to explode."

"I know. I've seen it happen." Hank shook his head with disgust. "So, if it doesn't work, why not stop?"

"The cartel won't let me."

"Afraid they'll kill you?"

"They have my son. They're wagering, sooner or later, I'll get it right." Manning slumped back against the table, as if the thought of his son with those evil men was more than he could bear.

"Where are they keeping your boy?" Bill glanced over at the woman, who was huddled in the corner like a tiny creature afraid of being eaten.

"Not far from here at an auto repair shop. They keep Ricky in a back office."

"How many are we talking?" Bill asked.

"I know of only seven."

"Does that include the two upstairs?" Hank said.

"Yes."

"Make it five." Hank realized he was still holding his gun. He slipped the revolver back into the holster.

"If you go in with a show of force, they'll kill Ricky for sure."

"Then we'll have to try another tactic," Hank said.

"I have an idea." Manning stood away from the

table. "It's a long shot, but it might just work."

"Let's hear it," Bill said.

* * *

The detectives staked out the auto repair shop across the street.

A burly guard patrolled the perimeter of the garage with one hand in the pocket of his bulky coat.

"Sure you don't want me to go along?" Bill peered out the window, keeping his head down.

"Better stay out here in case we need backup." Hank shrugged out of his suit jacket. He slipped his holster off his belt, unclipped his gold shield. Reaching down, he removed the holster for his backup piece from his ankle. He placed all the items on the seat.

The guard turned and marched the length of cyclone fence to the rear of the garage.

Hank glanced over the headrest at Manning, who sat in the backseat. "Ready?"

Manning took a deep breath. He gazed nervously out the window. "Yes, I think so."

Hank and the scientist got out of the car. They scurried across the street. The bay door remained open, so they ducked inside.

A lift kept a Mercedes sedan suspended six feet above the cement floor. Twin bays held two other luxury cars with their hoods up.

Hank and Manning didn't hear any pneumatic tools or the normal noises associated with the activities of an auto repair shop. It didn't appear that any mechanics were on duty. Fenders, doors, and various other exterior auto parts from different models of cars were stacked on metal racks in the chop shop.

"Where's the office?" Hank asked the scientist.

"Over there." Manning indicated a door farther back behind the cars.

Hank and Manning crept along a wall display of dangling radiator hoses and oval-shaped fan belts.

"Hands up!"

Hank immediately raised his hands. He glanced over his shoulder.

It was the guard from outside. The big man had the stealth of a cat. The muzzle of his Uzi machine gun pressed into the back of Manning's neck.

"We've got company!" the man hollered.

The office door flung open. Three men charged out. They rushed Hank, grabbing him roughly. They patted him down for weapons.

"Are they clean?" a voice called out from the office.

"Yes, Boss," said the thug with the Uzi.

Hank peered into the back room. A thin man wearing a black business suit sat behind a gray metal desk—hair greased back, a goatee, narrow beady eyes. His boney hand rested on the shoulder of a frightened boy seated next to him: Patrick Manning's son.

Hank's white dress shirt hung out of his waistband. They'd even turned the pockets of his slacks inside out.

"Hey, Boss!" The thug who had searched Manning held up two microchips.

The boss man got up from behind the desk. He ruffled the boy's hair the way an uncle might and stepped out of the office. His henchman handed him the micro-chips. The man studied the tiny objects, then shook his head. "Mr. Manning, you disappoint me."

"Please, let my boy go."

The boss man stared at Hank. "Who are you?"

"A friend of Patrick's."

"I smell a cop." The boss man nodded to a thug holding a pistol with a silencer. The man pointed his gun at the back of Hank's head, execution-style.

"On your knees."

Hank and Manning dropped to the floor.

"Perhaps it is time we severed our relationship." The boss man threw the chips at Manning. They bounced off his chest and landed on the floor in front of Hank.

"Ricky!" Manning shouted. "Son, I love you!"

Jumping off the chair, the boy cried out, "Dad! Dad! I want to go home!"

The boss man turned to block the boy's escape. The guy holding the pistol to Hank's head awaited instruction from his boss. The three other goons looked at each other with puzzled expressions.

The two microchips on the floor suddenly swelled, taking on the shape of Hank's service revolvers.

Hank snatched the newly materialized .38 snub-nosed with his right hand and grabbed the .380 automatic with his left. He raised his right hand over his shoulder and shot the gunman standing over him in the face. With both weapons pointing in opposite directions, Hank fired, dropping the thugs on either side.

The boss man reached for the gun tucked in his waist band.

IN CASE OF CARNAGE

Hank shot the ringleader in the chest.

The scrawny man fell back, crashing down on top of his desk.

"You're dead!" shouted the guy with the Uzi.

A loud gunshot rang out.

Hank watched the man drop his weapon and slam down on the floor.

Bill stood a few feet away, his arm fully extended, his gun smoking.

Ricky sprang into his father's arms.

"I got a little bored sitting in the car." Bill began to prod the bodies with the tip of his shoe.

"Thank God you didn't bring Sudoku. I can't believe this actually worked." Hank watched the relieved father clutching his son. "I'd hate to see what would happen if these microchips got into the wrong hands," Hank said. "Gunrunners and terrorists would have a field day, not to mention the military."

"What happens now?" Manning gave Ricky a tender kiss on the head.

"We'll make sure you and Ricky are set up in a witness protection program," Hank said.

"What about my research?"

"Is it worth your son's life?"

Manning hugged his boy.

* * *

Hank sat across from Jackie at the restaurant table. "I like your new dress." It was the same green as the last dress, which matched her eyes.

"Let's hope I don't get a stain. If my memory serves me, weren't you going to give me something?"

Hank took the gift out of his pocket and placed the small box next to Jackie's dinner plate.

She removed the lid and peeked inside.

"Here, I'll put it on." Hank jumped up from the table and went around behind Jackie's chair.

She handed him the necklace.

Hank draped the locket around her neck and cinched the clasp, then sat back down in his chair. "Like it?"

"Hank, it's lovely." Jackie held up the gold, heart-shaped locket. She pressed the catch, popping open the locket to look inside. She burst out laughing. "Hank, leave it to you."

A miniature photo was set inside each of the hinged hearts: one of Hank and the other of their golden retriever, Bella.

"Nice one of Bella, wouldn't you agree?"

"Hank, you're such a romantic."

"I'm glad you think so. So, am I forgiven?"

"I suppose. I guess it's true what they say."

"What's that?"

"Good things *do* come in small packages."

Or not, Hank thought to himself, unable to get those poor souls dead in the warehouse out of his mind.

3
CASE NUMBER: 18-02-238

Hank spotted a woman in a parka and jeans walking backwards on the opposite side of the road with her thumb out. "What is she thinking, hitchhiking way out here in the middle of nowhere?"

Bill slowed their unmarked sedan. He swung the car around onto the opposite lane to a complete stop on the shoulder.

Hank lowered his window. "Evening. You shouldn't be out here."

The woman froze, swinging the daypack off her shoulder. Mud caked her boots. She looked ready to bolt into the woods.

"It's okay. We're police." Hank showed her his badge. "Get in. We'll give you a ride."

The woman didn't move.

Bill leaned over the steering wheel. "Come on, lady. We have to go. We're answering a call."

The woman hesitated. She opened the rear door and climbed in behind Hank. She slowly edged the door closed.

Bill spun the car around and gunned the beefy engine down the rural road.

* * *

Two hours earlier . . .

"I used to love this drive this time of year." Fay slumped against the armrest. She wore her customary black slacks with the navy pea coat.

"It's still pretty." Will gazed out the windshield at the vibrant woodland kaleidoscope shades of yellows, oranges, and browns bordering the two-lane country road, shimmering in the late afternoon sun. Will wished he'd brought along the camera.

They traveled the sixty miles religiously, every Sunday, without exception. For Fay, admitting her mother to the convalescent home had been like opening the door for the Grim Reaper.

"How did she seem to you?" Fay asked.

It was the same question she asked during every weekly return trip from visiting her ailing mother. They could hardly be called "visits," as the woman seldom spoke or acknowledged their presence.

"She remembered my name." Watching Fay suffer as her poor mother sank deeper into dementia broke Will's heart even more than losing his mother-in-law, whom he loved as dearly as her daughter.

"No, she didn't."

"She certainly *did*."

"She called you Billy. That's my uncle. You've always been William."

"So, she forgot." Will cringed, regretting his choice of words. He glanced at Fay, hoping he hadn't upset his wife.

She stared down at her hands, which were clasped on her lap, her thoughts elsewhere. "She's getting worse."

Of course she is, Fay, Will thought. *Since when do Alzheimer's patients get better?*

"I'm sure the doctors are doing all they can," Will said. He knew the prognosis was grim. His mother-in-law would have been better off having cancer. At least then there might have been hope of it going into remission, perhaps even granting her the honorary status of a survivor. Not so with Alzheimer's. It was as good as a death sentence.

"They damn well better, for two thousand dollars a month," Fay snapped. She turned to glare out the window. Normally, she'd vent her frustration, blaming God for his unfairness, the doctors who were powerless to cure her mother, the inept orderlies, the emotionally draining weekly pilgrimages, the disease setting up roadblocks in her mother's confused brain, detouring her from Memory Lane. Instead she remained quiet.

Many times Will wished his mother-in-law would just die and save them from this purgatory.

Will noticed a car parked on the right shoulder of the road.

The front doors were open. He didn't see anyone

sitting inside or standing outside the vehicle.

Seemed strange someone would leave their car unattended on the side of the road for anyone to steal.

Will eased his foot off the accelerator. "Wonder where the owner is," he said, coming to a stop alongside the abandoned car.

"What are you doing?"

"They might be in trouble."

"This doesn't feel right."

"What if they need our help?"

"They probably got out to take a pee. Can we just go?"

"We should go see."

"No. Please, let's go."

"Fay, every Sunday it's the same damn thing. We're like prisoners in that godforsaken room. We're useless. There's not a thing we can do for her." Will motioned to the car. "There might be someone out there who desperately needs our help!"

Fay teared up. "Okay. But I'm staying in the truck."

Will turned off the engine. "I won't be long."

"Be careful."

Will brushed Fay's wet cheek. "Lock up after me."

He climbed out of the truck and closed the door.

Fay reached across to slap down the lock.

Will grabbed the tire iron from behind the cab.

He'd heard numerous stories about how criminals lured unsuspecting motorists.

One such tactic came to mind.

A motorist would spot a baby in a car seat on the shoulder of the road. The driver would pull over to investigate, only to discover it wasn't a real baby but a lifelike doll. Before the driver could trek back to their vehicle, a sinister figure would charge out of the bushes and assault them.

Will stepped around the tailgate, keeping one eye on the bushes at the edge of the woods. He cautiously approached the front of the car.

The late model Toyota Camry boasted a bug-splattered license plate.

Will placed his palm on the hood. The metal was still warm.

He stooped to glance inside the vehicle. His heart thumped in his chest.

A toddler's car seat perched in the back.

The sun had dropped behind the treetops, casting dark shadows across the road to where Will stood. He tapped the tire iron against the side of his leg.

He leaned in through the driver side, resting his elbow on the steering wheel. He saw a dark shape on the floor mat on the passenger side.

A rucksack.

He gazed down. A billfold had been left on the driver's seat.

Will reached for the wallet.

A hand grabbed his shoulder.

Will spun around so fast, he smashed his head on the doorframe. "Shit!"

"Honey? Are you okay?"

"Damn it, Fay. I thought you were in the truck." He massaged his head.

"I'm sorry. Did you find anything?"

"Yeah, someone left their wallet." He opened the

flap. "There's over two hundred bucks here."

"We have to call 9-1-1."

"Is the cell phone in your purse?"

"No. I thought *you* brought it."

"What's the point of even *having* the damn thing if neither one of us ever remembers to bring it?"

"We can have someone call when we reach the next gas station." Fay tugged on Will's arm. "What if there is some deranged killer out there watching us right now?"

"Then they'll get a piece of *this*." Will wielded the tire iron to show Fay he meant business.

"Now you're scaring me."

"There's nothing to be afraid of. I'll protect you."

"I want to go back to the truck."

"And wait by yourself?"

"Damn it, Will."

"At least let me give them their wallet. I can't just leave it in the car. Five minutes. If we don't find anyone, screw it. We'll leave."

"You promise?"

"Promise."

"Okay, but only for five minutes. Not a second longer."

Will stuffed the wallet in his coat pocket. They walked around the front of the car. He spotted an opening in the scrub brush. A worn trail led into the woods. He grabbed Fay by the hand and started down the path.

They hiked along the carpet of dead leaves, then stopped at the crest of a gulch. The embankment dropped off sharply into a gloomy hollow surrounded by dense briars.

The incline was a loose composite of sodden leaves,

soft loam, and slick mud. Hiking down would be difficult. Will hated to think what it would be like trying to climb back out.

"Hello! Anybody there?" he hollered down.

"Here!" a man yelled. "I'm down here! Please help me!"

"See? I was right." Will started to step down.

Fay clung to his arm. "Wait! It could be a trap!"

"I don't think so. *You* heard him. The guy's scared out of his mind."

"That makes *two* of us."

"Fay—"

Will's right foot slipped out from under him.

He dropped the tire iron, boot heels skidding down the slick mud. His fingers latched onto a tree root.

Fay was still clinging to his arm. She stumbled over Will, tumbling down into the shadowy hollow.

Will slid after her. Once he reached the bottom, he frantically looked around for Fay. It was almost nightfall. "Fay! Where are you?"

"Over here!"

Will turned to her voice. He could see her silhouette. She was kneeling on the ground, holding her left arm. "Are you hurt?" he asked.

A sinister figure suddenly loomed over Fay. The man hoisted a large rock over his head with both hands.

"Fay! Behind you!"

The rock came down like a sledgehammer, cracking Fay's skull open like a coconut. Her head lolled onto her shoulder. Blood trickled down her face like red paint dripping down the side of a can.

Fay teetered and fell onto the mulchy earth.

"No!" Will screamed. He charged, tackling the man. Will heard the air whoosh out of the man's lungs the moment he slammed him onto the ground.

Will straddled the gasping man, sinking his weight into his chest so the man couldn't catch his breath.

The man wheezed.

Will drove his fist into his face.

The man tried fending off another punch.

Will knocked his arm away, slugging him again. He kept beating him. His knuckles grazed the man's teeth. He struck him above the right eye. He heard bone crunch. He kept pummeling the man until his knuckles bled raw and his arms felt like lead weights.

The man's eyelids flittered.

Will's rage spurred him to curl his fingers around the man's throat. He pressed both thumbs on his Adam's apple.

His wife's killer drummed his heels into the ground.

Will throttled the life out of him.

Exhausted, he fell off the body.

Will crawled over to Fay.

He grasped her hand. Cold.

Her glazed eyes stared up at him.

Will broke down sobbing.

Something moved in the brush, startling Will.

"Who's there?"

A woman wearing a dark parka and jeans stepped out from behind the bushes. She stood silent, gazing down at the man with the bashed face. "Is he dead?"

"Yes. He killed my wife." His tone was unapologetic.

"We need to get out of here."

"What about my wife? I can't just leave her."

"You won't be able to carry her out. Not up *that* hill. Someone will come back for her."

They clawed their way up the steep slope. It was pitch dark by the time they came out of the woods.

Will looked at the woman. "You can follow me in your car."

"I don't think I'm in any shape to drive," she said.

"Fine. Ride with me." Will headed to the driver side of his truck. He unlocked the door with his key. The dome light came on the instant he opened the door. Will got behind the wheel and reached over to unlock the other door.

The passenger door swung open, and the woman scooted onto the bench seat.

"I believe I have something of yours." Will reached into his pocket. He passed the wallet to the woman.

She opened the billfold and smiled when she saw the money.

"You're lucky he didn't kill you," Will said, inserting the key into the ignition. He couldn't shake the image of Fay's body lying back in the woods. She had died because of this woman's poor judgment. "That was pretty stupid, stopping for a hitchhiker," Will said, his face flushed. He closed the driver door.

The interior light remained on.

Will glanced over. The passenger door was still open. He spotted something on the floor by her feet.

The rucksack.

He looked at the woman, suddenly realizing she had been the passenger, not the driver. She was the hitchhiker!

The woman gave him a sinister grin. "It's kind of ironic, him mistaking your wife for me." She aimed a small handgun at Will's face and pulled the trigger.

* * *

When the detectives arrived, they found two police cruisers parked on the opposite side of the road with their lights flashing. In front of the cruisers was the crime scene: a Toyota Camry with the front doors open and a pickup truck.

Bill pulled over to the shoulder and shut off the engine. He glanced over at the woman in the back seat. "Stay put. We'll get you a ride once we're done here."

The detectives exited the car. They strode across the road, switching on their flashlights.

"So, what do you have?" Hank flashed the officer his gold shield.

"Unconscious victim in the truck with a GSW to the head. It's amazing he's still alive."

Another officer came out of the woods, carrying a spotlight, his shoes and pants caked with mud. "There's a man and a woman down in a ravine, both bludgeoned to death."

Bill walked over to the car. He shined his flashlight inside. The light went out. He slapped the casing. Nothing. He turned to Hank. "We have any spare batteries?"

"Try the glovebox."

Bill marched across the road. He opened the driver door of the squad car and slid onto the front seat.

Hank shined his light inside the Toyota Camry. He

swept the beam over the child's car seat, panning over the clean upholstery and the spotless floor mats up front and back.

He turned to the truck and peered through the open passenger side to check on the wounded man who was slumped back on the bench seat, head resting against the rear window of the cab. To staunch the bleeding until the paramedic arrived, an officer had wrapped the man's head with a temporary dressing.

Hank kept the light out of the man's face.

The man's trousers and boots were covered with mud, along with the passenger floor mat.

"Ah, shit!" He raced to the front of the truck, looked across the road.

The light was on inside the Crown Victoria. Bill was stretched across the seat, looking inside the glovebox, unaware that the woman in the backseat was pointing a gun at the back of his head.

There was no time to warn him. Hank drew his service revolver, lined up the forty-foot long shot with a two-handed grip, and fired a single round.

The bullet shattered the rear side window. The woman jerked and fell back onto the seat.

Bill hopped out of the squad car. "Hank! What the hell?" He marched back across the road.

"Sorry. I didn't have time to warn you. I believe this is her handiwork. There was mud on her boots, same as on the passenger side of the truck."

"Good detective work, Columbo."

"Wish it had turned out better."

"Hey, look on the bright side."

"What's that?"

"Still have a partner."

"Do me a favor. Next time we teach a safety awareness class, remind me to mention it's never a good idea to pick up hitchhikers."

4
CASE NUMBER: 18-02-239

"This has been one helluva night." Bill kept fumbling with the knobs on the dashboard.

"Keep your eyes on the road. I'll do that." Hank fiddled with the temperature control. Warm air blasted from the vents.

"Nice of the sheriff to lend us a car, though I *do* miss the Crown Vic."

"Me too. Sure hated giving up my thirty-eight."

"All part of the investigation."

Hank gazed out the windshield. Driving through the woods at night was like passing through a poorly lit tunnel. "Can you put on the brights?"

"Tried. Doesn't work."

"Do you even know where we are?"

Bill slowed when they came to a fork in the road. "I'm a little turned around."

"Go left."

"You sure?"

"No."

Bill veered to the left. They traveled a couple more miles. The paved stretch turned to gravel. Further along, it became a dirt road.

"We should probably go back, find another way," Hank said.

"Yeah, I think you're—" Bill hit the brakes.

A white minibus loomed off the road a few yards ahead, its front end smashed into a large tree trunk.

The detectives exited the car. They spied patches of night through the treetops. They switched on their flashlights and shined them into the pitch-black woods, then on the distressed vehicle. The light refracted off the tinted windows. Each window was barred to prevent escape. No logos or lettering advertised a business or charter service anywhere on the vehicle.

Hank panned the light onto the open folding side door.

A dark, viscous liquid dripped from the bottom step onto the ground.

He crept down the shifting carpet of dead pine needles. He lost his footing and skidded down. He caught himself before slamming into the minibus.

"Careful there, Slick." Bill laughed.

Hank grasped the edge of the open bus door. He peered inside.

The driver was slumped over the steering wheel. The man's head looked like the inside of a watermelon after someone had punched through the rind.

Hank didn't see any damage to the dashboard. A single crack marred the windshield.

IN CASE OF CARNAGE

Blood dripped onto the top step, leaking out the end of a length of chrome handrail that had impaled the man through the ribcage. A steel screened partition separating the driver's seat from the passenger compartment had been forcibly bent forward and left hanging cockeyed on its hinges.

Hank ascended the steps, careful not to tread on the blood. He shined the light in the passenger compartment, then swept it to the left side of the aisle and over the first two sets of empty seats with a missing handrail. Then he swept to the next two rows, pointed the beam at the back seat by the emergency exit door, and returned the light back up to the front on the other side.

A woman screeched in his right ear.

Hank jumped back, slamming against the steel partition.

The loud cry faded.

"Hank!" Bill hollered down. "You okay?"

Hank turned to the source of the sound: a small TV and DVD player mounted on the mesh behind the driver's seat. On the screen, people shuffled single file across a fallen log in the dark. They either stumbled into a stream or into the waiting jaws of zombies on the shore.

"It's just a movie they were watching!" Hank answered.

The image flickered off. It flashed back on, obviously malfunctioning because of the crash.

Hank turned off the player.

A DVD case rested on top of the player. A screaming woman with big frizzy hair embellished the cover. An ensemble of enraged characters armed with primitive weapons and guns surrounded her. The title read: *Zombie Island Massacre.*

Hank backed out of the minibus. He climbed to the car.

"Anyone in there?" Bill asked.

"Only the driver. He's dead."

"Didn't his airbag go off?"

"Someone bashed his head in. You'd better call it in."

"Already tried." Bill held his cell phone up in the air, staring at the small screen. "No reception out here."

"Maybe there's a house up the road. We can use their phone."

They returned to the car.

A mile up, they found a two-story house overlooking a small lake. A string of shale steps led to a front porch with a wraparound redwood deck.

Hank knocked on the front door. The hinges creaked as the door opened a few inches. He crouched, drew his backup gun from his ankle holster. Bill took out his revolver.

"Hello?" Hank squeezed past the door. "We're the police! There's been an accident down the road. We'd like to use your phone!"

No one answered.

Hank turned to Bill. "Does this feel right to you?"

Bill shook his head.

The detectives stepped into a large living room.

Bill walked over to an end table. He looked down at the empty cordless phone dock. "Phone's gone."

Hank looked across the room.

On a big screen TV over the fireplace mantel, a football game played with the sound muted. A sectional couch faced the hearth. A person sat at the far end, head bouncing like a sports player bobblehead doll.

Bill stepped toward the couch. "Didn't you hear—"

A bloody hand appeared, its glistening red fingers kneading into the top cushion.

The detectives raised their guns.

A gruesome face rose, smeared with gore.

"Hands where we can see them!" Bill yelled.

The man snarled like a rabid dog, his face and shirt slick with blood. He sprang over the back of the couch.

Bill fired a single shot. The man's head snapped back. He fell against a standing lamp, knocking it over. He crumpled to the floor. The porcelain shade dropped on top of him, smashing to pieces with a loud crash.

Hank walked around to the front of the couch.

The man who had been bobbing his head sat slumped on the blood-drenched cushions, his face chewed beyond recognition.

"Ah, shit. He was eating this guy."

"Cannibals will do that."

"Bill, come on. Get real."

"All right. Would you rather I said 'zombie'?"

Hank shook his head. "Let's check the—"

A noise came from the kitchen.

Before they could take a step, another sound came from upstairs.

"You take the kitchen." Bill headed for the staircase.

Hank approached the kitchen entry. He edged along the wall, then saw a pair of bare feet on the floor with red toenail polish. He leaned forward till he could see the woman's legs, her hiked-up peach-colored skirt, a yellow sweater stained red . . .

And blood gurgling out of a hole that had been

savagely torn in her neck. A large clump of hair had been ripped from her scalp.

Hank stepped into the kitchen.

A man grabbed Hank by the shirt, knocking his gun from his hand.

They spun around, grappling like two roughhousing drunks.

The attacker's bloodshot eyes glared like two red-hot coals. He leaned in to bite Hank's face.

Hank punched him in the stomach. The man grunted, doubling over. Hank grabbed his assailant by the ears and rammed a knee into his face.

The man flew back, striking the base of his skull on a beveled edge of the countertop. He flopped to the floor, blood pooling onto the tile under his head.

A wild-haired man wearing blood-stained hospital pajamas charged out of the pantry.

Hank snatched a large cast-iron skillet that was dangling over the kitchen island. He gripped the long handle with both hands and swung at his attacker. The curved edge of the pan struck the crown of the man's skull, staggering him back. The top of his head was dented, like the cracked dome of a soft-boiled egg that had been tapped with a spoon.

The body hit the floor.

Hank picked up the .380 automatic. He rushed from the kitchen, dashed across the living room, and raced up the stairs.

He tried the light switch in the hallway. Nothing. Moonlight slivered through a window, casting eerie shadows on the walls.

IN CASE OF CARNAGE

Hank called out in a low whisper, "Bill?"

"In here."

Hank opened the first door on the right.

"Hurry—close the door!" Bill said.

Hank ducked into the room and locked the door behind him. When he turned, he saw Bill standing next to a boy who was seated at a desk.

"This is Jason," Bill said. "He lives here with his parents."

Jason looked about twelve years old, pudgy, a little nerdy in his thick-lens glasses.

"Did the zombies hurt my mom and dad?"

Hank nodded.

"I *hate* zombies! I *hate* them, I *hate*—"

"Calm down, little buddy!" Bill put an arm around the boy.

Hank walked over to the window. He peered between the curtains.

A figure stood on the deck, staring up at him.

Hank snapped the curtains shut. He turned around.

Bill was looking about the room like a pleased curator cherishing newly found relics.

"Hey, I like your room," Bill told Jason.

Zombie movie posters covered every wall: *Warm Bodies, Day of the Dead, Night of the Living Dead, Dawn of the Dead, Zombie High, I Am Legend, Resident Evil* . . .

Stacks of graphic novels and comic books crammed the shelves of a large bookcase. Bill grabbed a thick paperback volume. "Holy cow, kid! This is a compendium three of *The Walking Dead.*"

A DVD tower held a slew of low-budget zombie movie titles.

Zombie models adorned the dresser beside an army of grotesque action figures, which were huddled next to an autographed photo of the famous director George A. Romero wearing his signature black, large-framed spectacles.

On the bed, an Xbox wireless controller was nestled with a game box of *Nazi Zombies*.

Bill put the five-pound book back on the shelf. "I love your passion for zombies."

Jason backhanded a zombie figurine off his desk. "I *hate* them!" The plastic model smashed on the floor.

"Can't say as I blame you," Hank said, hoping to calm the boy.

Jason jumped up from his desk. He stormed over, ripped down a movie poster of Will Smith in *I Am Legend*. He crumpled it up into a ball and threw it down.

Hank looked about the room. "Is there a phone in here?"

"No." Jason returned to his desk. "There's a phone in my dad's den."

"Where's that?"

"Across the hall."

Heavy footsteps charged down the hallway outside. The doorknob rattled.

Hank turned to Jason. He put his finger to his lips, signaling the boy to be quiet.

The prowler stomped away in the direction of the stairs.

"Bill, stay with the boy."

"You get into trouble, yell," Bill said.

Hank quietly unlocked the door and opened it a crack to peer into the hall. "It's clear." The detective stepped out of the room, shut the door behind him, then darted across the hallway into the den.

A sliver of moonlight skirted between the curtains. Hank spotted the phone on the desk.

An arm wrapped around his neck and tightened like a hangman's noose. Hank gasped, attempting to break the choke hold with one hand. He could feel his windpipe being crushed. He was getting lightheaded. He let out a raspy breath, raised his gun . . .

A powerful swat knocked his weapon from his hand.

Hank stepped back, placing his right foot between his assailant's ankles in a feeble attempt to trip him up.

His attacker let go, spun Hank around, and head-butted him in the face.

Blood spewed from Hank's nostrils, pouring down his mouth and chin, soaking the front of his shirt.

The assailant shoved him back onto the desk.

Hank squinted.

His attacker approached with an open, savage mouth.

Hank swept his hand across the desk, searching the surface for a weapon. His knuckles brushed a plastic cup. He felt the pointy ends of a dozen pencils. He wrapped his fingers around the container and swung at the man's face.

The man jumped back, screaming. Quills of yellow no. 2 pencils quivered in his right eye socket.

Hank vaulted off the desk and drove his shoulder into the man's chest.

The man fell back, clutching Hank's arm.

Hank pulled away, his fingers snagging something from the man's wrist.

The man toppled over a credenza, crashing through a window. His body landed on the redwood deck with a dull thud.

Hank turned to the desk, picked up the phone, and punched three numbers.

"9-1-1 operator. What is your emergency?"

Hank opened his mouth. Nothing came out. His throat was on fire.

"Hello? Please state your emergency."

Again, it was too painful to speak.

Bill would have to make the call.

Hank looked down at his hand. He was clutching a white hospital bracelet. "Patient: 273B—Mission Psychiatric Clinic" was embossed on the identifier.

All this time, they'd been fighting deranged mental patients—*not zombies!*

That zombie movie on the bus must have caused them to go berserk. Hank wondered if Jason's love for zombies might be renewed once he learned that a crazed bunch of mental patients—not the undead—had killed his parents.

He shambled toward the doorway. He caught a glimpse of his reflection in a mirror on the wall. With his broken nose and bruised face, he hardly recognized himself. His shirt was ripped and covered in blood. His throat felt as if he had swallowed an entire jar of jalapeños.

He staggered out of the den and crossed the hall.

Hank opened Jason's door. The ceiling light was no longer on. He could just make out Bill shielding the boy, pointing his gun at the doorway.

Hank stepped into the dimly lit room.

"It's one of them!" Jason yelled.

Hank frantically shook his head.

Bill cocked the hammer.

"Shoot it!" Jason screamed.

Bill's finger stiffened on the trigger.

Hank tried to speak. It came out a croak—the sound a zombie might make just before a bullet scrambled its brain. He snatched his gold shield from his belt and tossed it across the room.

Bill took a quick glance at the object on the carpet. "Hank? Is that you?"

Hank shuffled across the room. He sat on the edge of Jason's desk, picked up a pencil, and wrote on a piece of drawing paper. He held the page up for the boy's benefit before turning it so Bill could read: I HATE ZOMBIES TOO!

5
CASE NUMBER:
18-03-240

A week later, Bill and another detective stood in the observation room, watching Officer Silverman through the one-way glass. Silverman escorted suspect Randolph Sikes into the claustrophobic interrogation room.

Sikes was a short man, approximately five feet, six inches tall, weighing somewhere around one hundred and eighty pounds, balding with curly brown hair on the sides, wearing his custodial uniform with black boots.

"Have a seat over there." Officer Silverman directed Sikes to a metal chair in the corner, his voice audible through the speaker in the observation room.

Sikes squeezed around the small table. He sat rigidly in the chair, hands folded on his lap.

"The detectives will be right in." Officer Silverman closed the door as he left the room.

Sikes took a moment to gaze about the tiny room, which was no larger than a jail cell. It was plain to see by the queasy expression on his face that he disliked the insipid lime-green paint on the walls, a nauseating color commonly found in convalescent home solariums and hospital wings for the mentally disturbed.

He stared suspiciously at the observation mirror, apprehensive of who might be concealed behind the reflective glass.

The detectives watched his every move, searching for signs that the man might have something to hide: the slightest twitch, a mannerism indicating reasonable guilt.

Sikes glanced nervously up at the stationary surveillance camera recording his every move.

He looked away, stared down at his shoes.

The floor tiles beneath his feet were black, creating the illusion that he was sitting over a dark pit—a psychological trick to rattle his subconscious, further his sense of powerlessness.

A fluorescent lamp was rigged to flicker overhead whenever the suspect was left alone in the room. The irritating strobe-like effect often induced headaches, rendering the suspect vulnerable. Once the interrogation began, a switch would be thrown to stabilize the light.

A brown phone with a crusty splotch resembling dried blood on the handset was mounted shoulder-high to the left of the door.

In addition to Sikes's chair, there were two other chairs which were ergonomically contoured, designed for extended periods of sitting. The chair facing Sikes was for the interrogator, while the chair on the other side of the six-foot-long rectangular table was for the witnessing detective.

The room was stifling, as the thermostat had been intentionally turned up. A strip of tape hung limply from the metal grate of the air-conditioning vent.

Sweat beaded on Sikes's forehead. He raised his hand to wipe his brow, exposing the damp ring forming under the armpit of his shirt.

He stared up at the camera, nervously pumping his left foot—squirming like he might wear a hole into the seat.

The two detectives stepped out of the observation room and strode down the hall to the next door.

Sikes jolted in his chair when the door opened.

"Mr. Sikes, I'm Detective Berg. This is Detective Hendrix." Berg sat in the interrogator's chair. He scooted the chair closer so his knees were almost touching Sikes's.

Bill sat in the other chair, observing Sikes from across the table.

Berg placed the police report on the table as if he had written it. Bill knew better. Hank had documented the case before taking administrative leave. Then Jonas Berg—"The Iceberg"—had swooped in with his uptown senior detective rank and taken over the investigation. Bill resented having to deal with the pompous cop who got off on upstaging his fellow officers.

Berg had served in the military. Rumors floated around that he'd been a ruthless interrogator at Guantanamo Bay and that there had been a cover-up concerning his methods for producing confessions.

Bill abhorred the idea of torturing a suspect. He could be intimidating in his own right. He had the exemplary arrest record to prove it and had never harmed a suspect during an interrogation.

He wondered what interrogation techniques Berg would employ.

Sustained isolation was generally a good way to break a person. Naked, blindfolded, left confined to the darkness with no human contact. So exhausted, they couldn't think straight. Sleep deprived, denied food and water. Sensitive parts of the body exposed to open flame. Waterboarding: pouring water over a restrained captive's hooded head, causing the prisoner to experience the traumatic sensation of drowning. The humiliation of being stripped of all humanity.

Bill kept a watchful eye on Berg.

Berg stared at Sikes, waiting for the man to look up from his shoes. "So, do you know why you were brought in?"

"Something to do with those women who were killed in our building, I suppose."

"That's right."

"Why ask me? I don't know anything."

"Do you like to be called Randolph or Randy?"

"Randolph. Only my mother calls me Randy."

"Okay, Randolph. So I gather you live with your mother?"

"No! I have my *own* place. At the Regal apartments."

"Where exactly?"

"The basement. I fixed up the storage room."

"Sounds nice. Is there anything you would like before we begin? Water or maybe some coffee? A cigarette perhaps? Smoking is generally forbidden. We can make a special exception in your case."

"I don't smoke."

"Just as well. It *is* a little stuffy in here."

"What's wrong with the air conditioner?" Randolph wiped his brow.

"Broken. We've got someone coming out to fix it. Maybe you would like some water?"

"Water would be good."

Berg glanced over at Bill.

Bill stood. He opened the door a few inches.

Officer Silverman was standing in the hall.

"You have that water?"

The recruit handed Bill the plastic water bottle he'd been holding.

"Thanks." Bill closed the door. He placed the drink on the table in front of Randolph. Bill sat down without saying a word.

Randolph picked up the bottle. He unscrewed the cap. He took a deep swig. He caught Bill's bulldog stare out of the corner of his eye. "Why is *he* here?"

"Detective Hendrix is here to assist me in the investigations of the murders of Nadine Simmons and Janice Kipper."

Bill glared at Berg.

"Am I a suspect?" Randolph's hand trembled as he put the plastic bottle on the table.

"Not necessarily. More of a person of interest."

"Just so you know, I have nothing to hide." Randolph squirmed in his chair.

"Why so fidgety?" Bill asked, considering himself as much a part of the interrogation.

"I've never been in a police station before."

Berg spoke in a calming voice. "I could see how it

might be intimidating. Relax. It'll all be over before you know it."

Randolph took a deep breath. He kept jiggling his foot.

"So, Randolph, I take it you're not a family man?"

"No, I live alone."

"Just for the record, what do you do at the Regal Arms Apartments?"

"Custodial work, light maintenance. I also take care of the landscaping."

"Mowing the lawn."

"That and—"

"So you must have the run of the place. Do you have master key, let's say, to the laundry room?"

"Yeah."

"What about to the tenants' doors?"

"If there's an electrical or plumbing problem they need me to fix, I go into their apartments when they're at work, so I don't disturb them."

"And the tenants trust you?"

"I'm bonded. I'm not going to steal anything."

"Well, I should *hope* not. Did you know Nadine Simmons?"

"I knew her."

"She was a resident at the Regal Arms for over ten years, correct?"

"Yeah, the old biddy," Randolph replied gruffly.

"I gather you didn't like her much."

"Not really."

"Why?"

"There was no pleasing her. She'd nag me every chance she got, bitching about everything. I'd be going up there almost every day, changing fuses. She'd want me to keep adjusting her thermostat because it was either too hot or too cold. I'd constantly have to unclog that damn toilet of hers."

"That must have driven you crazy."

"You bet it did."

"Isn't that your job? To fix things?" Berg gave Sikes a little shrug.

"She did it on purpose. There would have been nothing wrong with the thermostat if she had just left it alone. I don't know how many times I told her not to dump her damn cat litter down the toilet. She must have owned every imaginable kitchen appliance ever made. It was no wonder she kept blowing fuses."

"Well, the building *is* old."

"I keep it up."

"Ever wish Nadine Simmons would move out?"

"She was never going to move."

"Did she ever complain to the super?"

"About what?"

"You."

"What if she did?"

"Could be why you stabbed poor Mrs. Simmons in the laundry room. Don't you think it was rather mean, stuffing her body into the dryer?"

"I never killed her."

"Let's talk about Janice Kipper for a moment. You knew her, right?"

Randolph looked down for a second before replying. "Sure. Three-ten."

"Ever speak with her?"

"Sure, a few times."

"Ever been in her apartment?"

"Once, to replace a wall socket. She overloaded it with her computer stuff, almost caused a fire."

"Mind telling me where you were on . . ." Berg paused to flip open the file. He gave the report a quick perusal before continuing. "November fifth, between the hours of eight and twelve? The night Janice Kipper was strangled in her apartment." Berg slapped the file closed.

"I was downstairs watching TV."

Bill leaned across the table. "Was there anyone with you at the time who could corroborate your story?"

"No, I was alone."

Berg glared at Bill, a reminder that *he* was the one asking the questions.

"You're positive? You didn't leave for any reason?" Berg narrowed his eyes at Sikes.

"Like I said before, I was watching TV."

"You're sure?" Berg persisted.

"Yes! How many times do I have to tell you guys? What? You don't believe me?"

"Well, let me just say I've been doing this for some time now, interrogating suspects—"

"Wait a minute," Randolph interrupted. "I thought I wasn't a suspect!"

"Sorry, I meant in my line of work. There're a few things I've learned—like how to know when someone's lying."

"You mean like a lie detector test?"

"Well, not exactly. I can tell by the way a person reacts to a question. You know, their body language, facial expressions. Like, for instance, their eyes, which are always a dead giveaway. It has to do with how the human brain works. When a person is asked a question and tells the truth, the eyes always shift to the right. It's a subconscious reflex, like how your leg jumps when the doctor taps your knee with the little hammer—something beyond your control."

Bill wondered if Berg was exaggerating to intimidate Randolph.

Berg paused to lean forward. "But if the same person is asked a question and he lies, his eyes drift to the left. Strange how that works, wouldn't you say?"

"What does this have to do with me?"

"I've noticed your eyes have a tendency to shift to the left whenever you answer my questions." Berg placed his hand on Randolph's knee.

"I'm nervous, okay?"

"No, I think you're *lying*."

Randolph jerked away to escape Berg's touch. He tried scooting his chair back and hit the wall. "I swear, I'm telling the truth."

"Randolph, please. Don't insult my intelligence."

"Shouldn't I be getting a lawyer?"

"Are you asking for one?" Bill asked. He knew if Randolph insisted that an attorney be present, Berg would have to honor his request, ending the session.

Randolph paused to gather his thoughts.

"If you're innocent, you should have nothing to hide," Berg said. "Asking for a lawyer suggests otherwise." Berg edged his chair a little closer.

"But I didn't do it. I keep telling you, I was in my room!"

"There you go again, looking to the left."

"I can't help it! I'm scared!"

"Your eyes. They'll betray you every time."

"I get this tic when I'm nervous. Can we just stop? I need to think." Randolph rested his elbows on his knees, burying his face in his hands. He rocked slightly, muttering to himself.

Berg leaned forward. "Let's just say, hypothetically, you *did* kill Janice Kipper."

Randolph raised his head. "But I just told you—"

Berg stuck out his palm, silencing Randolph. "Please, just humor me for a moment. If you did, we would need to substantiate your guilt, wouldn't you say?"

Randolph gave the detective a wary nod. He picked up his bottled water.

"From our forensic reports, we know the killer is right-handed."

Randolph looked gloomily at the plastic bottle in his right hand.

"Our profiler believes the killer is antisocial, most likely an introvert, a loner, much like you."

"Since when is living by yourself a crime?"

"No one said it was. It's also suggested the killer has a score to settle and hates women. Do you hate women, Randolph?"

"No!"

"So, let me take a wild guess. You let yourself into her apartment when she wasn't there. Tampered with . . . what? A light switch? Messed up her toilet so you would have to come up to fix it?"

"I did no such—"

"Randolph! You took the master key from the cabinet in the storage room, snuck in, came up behind Janice Kipper, and strangled her!"

"No, I didn't!"

Bill slid the case folder over to himself and flipped through the pages.

"Did it make you feel like a man?" Berg was having fun. "Did it get you off?" He clamped his fingers like a vise on Randolph's right kneecap.

Randolph grimaced, tears rolling down his cheeks. "Let go! You're hurting me!"

"I know. It's amazing what a little bit of pressure can accomplish." Berg squeezed harder.

"Please stop!" Randolph yelled.

"Come on, Randolph! Confess!"

Bill had seen enough. "Let him go, Berg!"

Berg lifted his hand. He pushed back his chair.

"I'm going to be sick!" Randolph clutched his stomach. He put his head between his knees.

Bill stood and opened the door. "Better get him to the restroom before he pukes!"

Officer Silverman hurried in. He collected Randolph as he began to gag and ushered him from the room.

"Well, it won't be long now." Berg sat back in his chair with a big grin on his face.

Bill frowned. "You really think Randolph is our killer?"

"Guilty as sin."

"Anyone who knew where the master key was could have taken it."

"He's our man. You watch. When he comes back, I'll squeeze a confession out of him."

Bill glanced down at the case folder. "You read my

partner's report in its entirety?"

"Pretty shoddy police work. Be happy I solved your case for you."

"You *did* read that Janice Kipper worked for your police station uptown? Her job was transcribing cold cases, which she did mostly from her apartment."

"So?"

"Ever meet her?" Bill sat back, crossing his arms.

"Sure, in the morgue."

"You know, there's no mention of the master key in my partner's report."

"So, what of it?"

"How'd you know where it was?"

"Randolph must have mentioned it."

"No, he didn't."

"So, what are you implying, detective? That *I* killed those women?"

"Might explain why you suddenly wanted to take over this investigation—steer it in the wrong direction."

"That's absurd."

"Is it? Were you afraid Janice Kipper was going to come across something incriminating about you in one of those cold cases? A loose end, perhaps?"

"I'd stop if I were you," Berg threatened.

"You thought by murdering Nadine Simmons you would throw us off, make us think there might be a serial killer loose, when *you* strangled Janice Kipper. Nice touch."

"You're out of your mind."

"Am I?"

"I'm warning you, Hendrix. One more word—"

"Tell me I'm wrong."

"You're wrong!"

"You didn't kill Nadine Simmons and Janice Kipper?" Bill persisted.

"No! I didn't!" Berg replied indignantly.

"Then why do you keep looking to the left?"

6
CASE NUMBER: 18-03-241

Hank and Jackie were walking Bella by the fenced-off community pool when Hank spotted something in the street next to the curb. He reined Bella in and bent down to retrieve the item.

"What did you find?" Jackie stared at the laminated card in his hand.

"A Kaiser Permanente medical card belonging to a person named Kelly Rice."

According to the card, Kelly was a twenty-year-old female.

Jackie gazed down at the pavement bordering the curb. "There're more."

Hank handed the looped end of Bella's leash to Jackie. He started collecting more of the cards, which were scattered on the side of the street. He gathered up a State Farm insurance card, a dental card with Kelly's name on it, a library card, a San Jose State University student ID card with her name and picture, along with a membership card for the YWCA.

"Someone must have stolen her purse," Hank said, "tossed out what they didn't want, and kept her driver's license and credit cards."

"Poor girl must be frantic." Jackie gave Bella some slack to sniff the base of a tree.

"I'd hate to see her become a victim of identity theft." Hank stooped to pick up a book of matches with "Third Street Bar & Grill" stenciled on the front. He flipped open the cover. The pack was full with a handwritten phone number on the inside flap. He slipped the matches into his trouser pocket.

* * *

On the way back to the house, Jackie glanced over at Hank. "You don't think anything happened to her?"

"What do you mean?"

"I don't know. Maybe she's hurt."

"Most likely she pulled up to a light," Hank said, "and some guy opened the passenger door and snatched her purse off the seat. Happens all the time. This is why I'm always bugging you to keep your doors locked when you're out by yourself."

"What if they stole her car?"

"Jackie, I'm sure she's fine."

* * *

When they returned home, Hank got on the phone

to notify the police. Normally, he would have called Bill at the station, but as Hank was on administrative leave pending the Internal Affairs investigation of the hitchhiker shooting, he thought he would do what any law-abiding citizen would do and dial the non-emergency contact number 3-1-1. He spread the cards out on the kitchen counter.

When the dispatcher answered, Hank explained that he'd found identification cards belonging to someone else and wanted them returned to their rightful owner. The dispatcher told Hank a patrol car would be sent over. After a couple more questions, he thanked Hank for taking the initiative to call it in. Hank never mentioned he was a cop. He hung up the phone.

Ten minutes later the phone rang. Hank answered. A woman told him she was outside to pick up the ID cards.

"That was fast!" Hank hung up. In his haste to scoop up the cards, he swiped most of them onto the floor. He gathered the spilled cards and the ones still on the counter, then raced from the kitchen through the living room, dodging furniture like a slalom skier. He bolted out the front door.

A police cruiser waited at the end of the driveway. Hank handed the short stack of plastic cards through the open window to the female police officer. As he'd never personally worked with the officer, he introduced himself as a fellow cop.

"Where did you find these?" she asked.

"By the Cabana Club."

The officer pulled up a GPS map on her computer screen. Hank pointed to the street where they'd found

Kelly Rice's property.

The officer thanked him, and Hank watched the patrol car pull away.

* * *

Hank sat at the kitchen table. Jackie dried a glass and put it away in the cabinet. She hung the dish towel on the oven handle. She studied him for a moment, then asked, "What's with the look? Is something wrong?"

"Now you've got *me* doing it. I can't stop thinking about the girl."

That evening, Hank and Jackie stayed up later than usual to watch the Eleven O'Clock News, managing to stay awake for the thirty-minute broadcast.

When the news ended, Hank switched off the television. "Well, no reports of a missing person."

Jackie took a deep breath. "Thank God." She got up from the couch and traipsed off to bed.

Hank stared at the blank TV screen. He was dead tired, but he knew he wouldn't sleep. He turned off the lights and followed Jackie upstairs.

* * *

The next morning, Jackie stood at the stove, watching four eggs bobbing about in a pot of boiling water. Hank sat at the kitchen table, flipping through the morning-edition newspaper without purpose. Finally, he gave up. He closed up the paper, folded it, and slipped the rubber band back on like the paperboy. He tossed it on the table and said, "I think we should try contacting Kelly Rice ourselves."

"Maybe she's listed." Jackie turned off the burner. She went over to the table, pulled out a chair, and sat next to Hank.

Reaching from his chair, Hank pulled open a cabinet drawer. He took out the telephone book and placed it on the table.

"Hank, why don't we just go on the Internet and look her up? Wouldn't that be faster?"

"Not necessarily. The phone book offers a shorter, more organized list, and we won't have to deal with popup ads trying to sell us something and slowing down our search. If this doesn't pan out, then we'll try the Internet." He opened the directory to the residential section under "R." He saw an entire column of customers with the last name "Rice." None with the first name "Kelly," though there were three with the first initial "K."

Hank dialed the first phone number, while Jackie leaned in to listen.

"Hello?" a tired voice answered.

"I was wondering if I may speak with Kelly."

"Who?"

"Kelly Rice."

"You must want Karen."

"Sorry, I must have the wrong number."

Hank tried the second number.

"Yeah?" a man answered.

"Hi, I'd like to speak to Kelly."

"This is Kelly. Who the hell is this?"

Hank hung up.

"That was rude." Jackie made a goofy face.

"Last one." Hank punched in the phone number.

This time they hit pay dirt when Hank asked for Kelly.

"What do you want her for?" the grumpy woman snapped.

"Can I please talk to Kelly?"

"Not likely."

"Why not?"

"Who did you say you were?"

"If you let me speak to her, I'll explain."

"Look, whoever you are, I'm busy."

"We found some of Kelly's things."

"What things?"

"Her ID cards. We think someone might have stolen her purse."

"Is this a sick joke? My mother never lost her purse. It's in her room in the closet."

"Your mother is Kelly Rice?" Hank's eyes beamed.

"My mother is dead, asshole! Who the hell is this? I'm calling the . . ."

Hank lowered the phone from his ear, ending the call.

Jackie gave Hank a loving pat on the arm. "That was a bit of a bust."

"I'll say."

"If Kelly is a college student, couldn't she be living at home with her parents?"

"It's worth a shot." Hank used the house phone while Jackie called on their cell phone. It took two hours to call every resident with the last name "Rice" listed in the phone book.

After they were through, they compared notes. Nine

of the numbers were no longer in service. Twenty-seven had gone directly to voice mail. Hank and Jackie had left short messages with a number to call. Fourteen had kept ringing, no one picking up. The residents they *had* talked to knew no one by the name Kelly.

Hank slumped back on the couch. "That was a big goose egg."

"Maybe she's from out of town or doesn't have a phone."

"She'd have a cell phone. Being a college kid, she must use the Internet."

"I'll bet she's on Facebook."

Hank went into the den. He booted up the computer.

After an extensive search on Facebook, they found a slew of women doing selfies in skimpy outfits, a television anchorwoman, a guy with a beard reaching his belt, and an actress from the television series *Lost*, all listed as Kelly Rice. None of them looked anything like the picture on Kelly's SJSU student ID.

"Maybe you should give Bill a call?"

"I'd hate to bug him. He's been tied up with that double-murder case."

"You never know. He might have heard something."

"All right. I'll call him in the morning."

* * *

Hank called Bill at eight sharp and told him about finding the cards in the street. "Have you heard of anyone reporting someone by the name of Kelly Rice missing?"

"No," Bill said. "I'll check with Missing Persons."

"I'd appreciate it."

"I have some good news. Cracked our two homicides."

"Who was it?"

"Remember Berg from uptown? I tripped him up during our interrogation. He was trying to frame the apartment handyman. After we booked Berg, I checked his phone history. Turns out Berg had been calling Janice Kipper. She must have come across a cold case implicating Berg in a crime, so he killed her. He murdered Nadine Simmons to throw us off."

"Glad to hear someone finally thawed out that dick Iceberg," Hank said.

"I'd better get back to work," Bill said. "I'll call you if I learn anything about the girl. When are you coming back?"

"Soon, I hope. Still waiting for the all clear on the hitchhiker shooting."

"Give my love to Jackie."

"Will do. See ya." As they had an answering machine, Hank saw no reason to hang around the phone. "Put on your coat," he told Jackie. "We're going to the park."

Jackie hung up her apron. She clapped her hands. "Bella, want to go for a *walk*?"

The dozing golden retriever's ears perked. She scrambled to her feet on the polished kitchen floor, nails clicking as her pads sought traction. As soon as she reached the carpeted living room, she bolted for the front door to wait.

Out on the walk, Hank took the leash, knowing Bella would be like a team of horses, pulling him along once she sensed they were going to the nearby park.

IN CASE OF CARNAGE

Hiking down a designated path to the meadow area where Bella could romp off-leash, they noticed two police cruisers blocking a service road. An officer wrapped the end of a long barrier of yellow police tape around a tree trunk. A middle-aged couple wearing matching blue jogging outfits stood behind the tape, rubbernecking. Two officers stood on a footbridge, leaning over the railing, looking at something down in the washed-out gulch below.

Hank held Bella back, afraid she might jump on the curious people. He stood by the man, watching the police. "What's going on?"

"They found a body," the man said. "I heard one of them say it's a woman."

***

Jackie was staring in the refrigerator deciding what to cook for dinner, when Hank suggested they watch the afternoon news report for any word on the woman found in the park.

Jennie Lee, Hank's favorite female news reporter, was on the scene, microphone in hand, standing in the park just outside the yellow police tape. "Police have yet to determine the cause of death of a woman found dead under a pedestrian bridge in Holly Park. The woman's identity has not been released. Stay tuned for further developments in this story. This is Jennie Lee reporting."

Jackie put her hand up to her mouth. "It's her, isn't it?"

"There's a good chance." Hank wished he'd been able to see the body for himself, but he knew his captain

83

would object if he got involved in an ongoing investigation while on administrative leave.

After dinner, Jackie was sweeping the kitchen floor when she called out to Hank. "Honey! Look what I found!"

Hank came in from the living room.

Jackie held up Kelly Rice's Kaiser Permanente card. She laid the card on the kitchen counter.

"Where was that?" Hank asked.

"Under the cove. You must have missed it when you were picking the cards off the floor."

"I'd better call it in!"

"Hank, it's getting late. Do it tomorrow."

"All right, but I still think it wouldn't hurt to call now." Hank placed the card on the kitchen counter next to the phone, then went back into the living room.

He sat on the couch, switching on the television with the remote.

Jennie Lee stood in front of a glass-faced building. "We have just learned that the woman found in Holly Park was Claudia Danker, age thirty-five, a prominent real estate broker with Midtown Properties. An investigation is still under . . ."

Hank turned off the television and rushed into the kitchen. "It wasn't her after all."

"What?" Jackie leaned the broom against the side of the refrigerator.

"Kelly Rice. She wasn't the woman they found in the park."

"Oh, thank God."

Hank looked at Kelly's medical card on the counter.

He felt something in his trouser pocket and pulled out the matchbook he'd found in the street. "I wonder if these matches belonged to Kelly." He opened the flap, looked at the handwritten phone number inside. He grabbed the house phone and punched in the number.

The phone on the other end rang repeatedly before a woman's voice came on the line.

"Hi! I can't come to the phone right now, but if you would like to leave a message, I'd be more than happy to return your call. Please wait for the beep. Bye now."

Hank waited for the beep, then said, "My name is Hank Jenkins. You don't know me, but I have something of yours and would like to return it. Please call me back." Hank left his phone number, then ended the message.

A minute later, the phone rang.

"Hello?" Hank answered.

No reply.

"Hello?" Hank gazed over at Jackie.

"Who is it?"

"I don't know. They won't say anything." Hank swore he could hear shallow breathing. Someone was definitely on the line. "Hello, this is the police. I'm looking for—"

The other end went dead.

"Damn."

"What's wrong?"

"They hung up." Hank looked at Jackie. "It just dawned on me. If Kelly's purse was stolen, the thieves probably kept her phone. That was probably *them*."

"You don't know for certain."

"Jackie, I left my name! We're listed! Shit!"

"That's not good," Jackie said, shaking her head.

"Maybe you should call Bill."

"No, not yet. We need to be a hundred percent sure."

"So what do we do?"

Hank stared at the Third Street Bar & Grill matchbook in his hand. "When's the last time I took you out to lunch?"

***

The next day, Hank parked on the fourth level in the Third Street garage so they wouldn't have so far to walk to the restaurant. They rode the elevator down. Once they were on the sidewalk, Jackie looped her arm in the crook of Hank's, and they strolled down the street.

They passed an automobile repair shop. A loud torque wrench screeched to an abrupt stop. The cars waiting for service were beat-up wrecks with faded paint jobs, better candidates for the compactor than an overhaul.

Hank spotted two rough-looking characters wearing dark sunglasses and hooded sweatshirts; they were standing by a black van that was tucked in the alley beside the shop. The men seemed to take a special interest in Hank and Jackie, then climbed in their van.

Hank and Jackie walked for another block, then stopped in front of a run-down house with a bank-owned foreclosure sign staked into the weedy front lawn. A clear plastic box was mounted on the post under the "For Sale" sign, jammed full of pricing flyers.

Hank took a single-page advertisement and gave it a quick look. "We could swing this."

"You'd want to live down here?"

IN CASE OF CARNAGE

"I meant, as a second property for a rental, it's not bad." Hank shrugged, then folded the flyer and stuffed it in his back pocket.

A little farther down stood the Third Street Bar & Grill, a small hideaway with a brick, wrought-iron facade, wedged between a secondhand clothier and a thrift store. A green canopy shaded the small tables and chairs on the patio area, which was bordered with potted ferns. An outdoor bar served customers who were seated outside.

Hank and Jackie sauntered through the gate. They sat at the bar.

The young bartender sported a tanning-booth tan, a shaved head, and a diamond stud in each earlobe, the three top buttons on his floral shirt open to show off the bling on his hairless chest.

"What can I get you folks?" The bartender placed two cork coasters on the bar.

Hank looked at Jackie. "Care for a pomegranate margarita?"

"I'd love one."

"Make that two."

"Coming right up." The bartender scooped ice into a blender and grabbed two bottles from a shelf under the bar.

Hank plucked a matchbook from a woven basket. He took the matches out of his trouser pocket. They looked the same.

Shortly after, the bartender placed two wide-mouthed, long-stemmed glasses with straws on the bar top. The rims were dashed with salt. Lime wedges floated on the surfaces of the alcoholic beverages.

Jackie took a sip of her margarita.

"Careful you don't get a brain freeze," Hank warned, taking a drink.

"Would you like lunch menus?" the bartender asked.

"Please." Hank licked the salt from his lips.

The bartender grabbed two menus from a stack by the register and placed them on the counter.

Jackie opened her menu to peruse the luncheon specials. She glanced over her shoulder. "Uh-oh, trouble."

Hank spun around in his seat.

Three attractive women drifted into the patio area. They sat at a nearby table, dumping their big, long-strap purses on the flagstone.

The bartender swaggered over to the women's table. He said something to the women, making them laugh.

"Quite the lady's man," Hank quipped.

"So it would seem."

The bartender kept laying on the charm.

Hank returned to his menu.

Jackie was wavering on a third pick when the bartender returned.

"Have you decided?"

Jackie stared at the menu. "I think I might need another minute."

"No rush."

"I guess we picked a good time to come." Hank gestured to the empty tables.

"Come here at night," the bartender said. "The place is crazy. Wednesday's ladies night. Drinks are half price for the women."

"Bet *you* do all right." Hank gave the bartender a

conspirator's grin.

"I get my share."

Jackie struggled to keep a straight face.

Hank opened the matchbook. He showed the bartender the phone number that was scrawled inside the flap. "Any chance you might recognize this number?"

The bartender started to laugh. "I remember who *wrote* it."

"Was her name Kelly Rice?"

"She never gave her name."

"When was this?"

"I don't know. Maybe five or six days ago. She was trying to slip me her number. To tell you the truth, she wasn't my type. I told her I already had a girlfriend. She just shrugged it off, put the matchbook in her purse. I think she was used to rejection."

"That's sad. We were hoping you might be able to help us. We have something of hers we wanted to return."

"Funny you should say that." He reached down behind the counter. "She left this on the bar last time she was here." The bartender handed Hank a compact digital camera. "Maybe, when you find her, you can give it back to her. I'm afraid someone's going to walk off with it." He jotted down their order and meandered to the kitchen.

Hank studied the camera in his hand. "She seems to be losing stuff left and right." He leaned over his margarita and took a long pull on his straw. A second later, his eyes snapped closed. He clamped his hand over his forehead.

"Hank? Are you all right?"

"Brain freeze."

***

Lying on their bed in the master bedroom, Hank scrolled through the photos on the small screen on the back of the digital camera.

Jackie finished brushing her teeth. "Find anything interesting?" She climbed into bed, grabbing her novel off the nightstand.

"It's strange. I haven't seen one picture of a person. I must have gone through a hundred photos. It's all interior shots of different homes."

"That's odd." Jackie opened her latest Dean Koontz thriller.

Hank turned off the camera. He slipped it into the drawer of his nightstand. He looked over at Jackie. Her eyes were drooping. "Want me to turn off the light?"

"Okay." She put the book back on the nightstand.

Hank switched off the light.

Sometime in the night, Hank startled out of a deep sleep to the sound of silverware rattling in a kitchen drawer downstairs and Bella barking.

He jumped out of bed, waking Jackie.

"What's wrong?" Jackie asked. "Why's Bella barking?"

Hank reached into his nightstand drawer and withdrew his personal revolver, which he kept for home protection. "Call 9-1-1." He stepped from the bedroom and crept down the stairs.

He entered the kitchen, switching on the light.

IN CASE OF CARNAGE

The sliding glass door leading to the backyard stood wide open.

Bella growled at a man in a hooded sweatshirt who was scowling from the other side of the kitchen table.

"What the hell are you doing in my house?" Hank hid his gun near his hip.

"Where is it?" the man demanded.

"Where's what?"

"The camera."

"Why do you want it?"

"Hand it over, or else there'll be—"

"Hank! I've called the police!" Jackie hollered down from upstairs.

Hank stepped forward and grabbed Bella's collar. She kept barking.

"Bella, quiet!" Hank shouted firmly. Bella snarled at the man.

Another man in dark clothes loomed in the backyard.

Bella lurched, tugging Hank off balance and providing just the distraction the intruder needed to bolt out the door.

"They called the cops!" the man yelled, and they fled through the backyard.

Hank heard them scrambling over the front fence.

He closed the sliding glass door and locked it. He ran from the kitchen, rushing to the living room window and spotted a black van parked in front of the house.

The two men jumped into the vehicle. The driver cranked the engine, but it wouldn't start. As sirens approached, they scurried from the van. Two patrol cars stormed down the street. The men scrambled to escape, only to be boxed in. With nowhere to go, they threw their hands in the air and dropped to their knees.

* * *

Bill sat in Hank's favorite armchair. He pulled a cell phone out of an evidence bag, stretched his arm across the coffee table, and showed it to Hank and Jackie. "Found this in the van." He punched in a series of numbers.

The phone in the kitchen rang.

Hank started to get up.

Bill held up his hand. "It's only me."

Jackie clutched Hank's arm. "So, they *did* have Kelly's phone."

"Kelly?" Bill placed the phone back in the evidence bag.

"Kelly Rice." Hank stared at Bill. "The girl I told you about."

"Oh, yeah."

"We have more of her stuff. Hold on. I'll go get it." Hank raced out of the room.

A few moments later, he returned to the living room with the camera, Kelly's medical card, and the matchbook. "Her number's written inside the matches. We believe this is her camera."

Bill opened the matchbook. He looked at the phone number, shaking his head. "I take it you heard about the dead woman found in the park."

Hank nodded. "Yes, it was on the news."

"The number in this matchbook belongs to Claudia Danker. This is her phone."

"I don't understand." Hank turned to Jackie. They

exchanged wide-eyed looks.

"After the officer left your house, she drove to where you found those ID cards. She got out on foot and combed the area. She came across more discarded items in the street, only they had Claudia Danker's name on them, suggesting her purse had been rifled through before her body was dumped in the park. Apparently, they were looking for this." Bill held up the camera.

"One of those guys who broke in wanted me to hand over the camera."

"Apparently, they were growing marijuana in one of the foreclosed properties down on Third Street. They saw a real estate woman taking pictures next door, thought she was going to blow the whistle on their little operation. They killed Claudia Danker the next day when she came back. But they never found the camera. Where was it?"

"She left it at the bar down the street."

"I guess this wraps it up."

"Wait a minute. What about Kelly Rice? Did you ever find her?"

"No one's reported her missing." Bill pushed out of the armchair. "I guess I'll be shoving off."

After Bill left, Hank called Bella, and they followed Jackie back upstairs to bed.

* * *

The following morning, while Hank took his shower, Jackie prepared a late breakfast in the kitchen. She switched on the small portable TV on the counter. On the screen, Jennie Lee clutched her microphone: "Two boys taking a shortcut to school through a wooded area in Holly Park were extremely traumatized when they stumbled upon the body of a young woman in a ravine only days after Claudia Danker was found murdered in the same park. Police are withholding the victim's identity upon notification of the nearest of kin. This is Jennie Lee reporting."

7
CASE NUMBER: 18-03-242

Hank looked like a bum in his grubby, paint-spattered sweatshirt, raggedy jeans, and grungy sneakers. His hair was slightly mussed, and he had two-day stubble on his face. His hands were grimy from prepping the walls and cleaning the brushes and rollers after painting the living room and the den.

They'd been up early moving furniture, masking the trim—all the preparations before tackling the job. It was early evening by the time they finished rehanging pictures, putting everything back in place. Worn out, Jackie didn't feel like cooking and wanted only to soak in the tub.

Hank suggested takeout, maybe Chinese. Jackie was in the mood for orange chicken and honey-walnut prawns.

While Jackie went upstairs to pamper herself, Hank grabbed his wallet and keys. He opened his billfold and saw he was low on cash. He needed to stop at the ATM to withdraw money to pay for dinner.

Hank drove to the mall through light weeknight traffic and parked in a spot closest to the food court entrance. Twenty feet down the sidewalk, an ATM glowed outside the bank where Hank kept his account. He switched off the engine, turned on the overhead light, and withdrew his wallet from his back pocket. His debit card reflected in the light.

A few months ago, Hank and Bill had taught a community self-awareness class to a group of senior citizens, warning them of the dangers of using an ATM, especially at night.

Always lock the door after leaving the car, or bring a friend. Never approach an ATM where suspicious characters lurk. Avoid using an ATM shrouded by shrubbery where a mugger might hide. Never use an ATM that is not safely illuminated at night. Always have your debit card in your hand before stepping out of your car, so you won't be distracted searching in a wallet or digging through a purse. These were all perfect opportunities for a criminal to catch you off guard.

Of course, Hank's bank adhered to all the safety precautionary measures, including installing a security camera and a panic button on every ATM, should a customer be assaulted.

Hank grabbed his keys out of the ignition. He noticed a woman standing fifty feet away at a different bank's ATMs. She fumbled through her purse, most likely struggling to find her debit card under the flickering fluorescent lights.

With no vehicles at the curb, Hank wondered where she'd parked. He leaned forward to discover a white van parked a few yards from the kiosk.

Hank kept watching the woman.

A man wearing a black ski mask stepped out from behind the front of the van. He rushed the woman, punching her in the face. Then he grabbed the strap of her purse and ripped it from her shoulder.

"Hey!" Hank yelled, unsnapping his seat belt, never once taking his eyes off the attack in progress.

The assailant shoved the woman to the sidewalk.

Hank leaped out of his car.

The man crouched. He grabbed the woman's right wrist.

Hank saw him holding something in his other hand.

The woman screamed.

"Police!" Hank bellowed, running toward them, wishing he had his gun.

The mugger turned. He sprang to his feet and bolted behind the van.

Hank sprinted to the hysterical woman. "Everything is going to be fine. I'm a cop."

"My God! My hand!" The woman clutched her right hand, blood seeping out between her fingers.

"Try and stay calm." Before Hank could attend to the woman, he needed to be sure the mugger wasn't skulking behind the side of the van, waiting to attack again. He braced himself, edging around the front bumper. He snuck a peek.

The man was gone.

The crying woman paused to catch her breath. Hank heard rapid footfalls fading into the shadows.

Hank returned to the woman.

Blood continued to gush from her hand.

Hank slipped his sweatshirt up over his head. He turned it inside out. "Let me wrap your hand."

"Oh, God, it hurts!"

"You're lucky I showed up when I did." He gently pried her protective hand from her injured hand. Blood spurted from the stump.

Hank glanced about the sidewalk for the missing digit, appalled that her attacker had run off with her severed thumb.

* * *

"Talk about a disgrace to the department," Bill said, commenting on Hank's shabby appearance.

"Yeah, I guess I do look a mess." Hank watched the paramedics push the woman on the collapsible gurney into the back of the ambulance.

"This makes the fifth one this week." Bill closed up his notepad.

"She told me he cut her thumb off with a pair of pruning shears."

"Sounds like our guy. I understand you got the call."

"The investigation cleared me. I'll be back tomorrow."

"Don't forget the donuts."

* * *

The New Age Banking corporate office was downtown in the financial district.

The detectives rode the elevator up to the 37th floor and approached the reception desk. "We're here to see Mr. Stanton.”

"He's expecting you. Please go through those doors.”

The CEO of NAB got up from his desk to greet them as they came into his office. “Please, gentlemen. Have a seat. Can my secretary get you anything?”

"No thanks.” Bill grabbed a chair facing the front of Stanton's massive desk. Hank sat in the chair next to Bill.

"How may I help you?” Stanton sat back behind his desk.

Bill took the lead. “Maybe you could tell us a little bit about your company. I understand it's very innovative.”

"At New Age Banking, we like to pride ourselves as one of the most efficient, cost-effective institutes in the country. For example, we no longer send our customers their billing statements through the mail. Everything is electronic. By eliminating postage, printing, and man power, we were able to save the company one million dollars a year.”

"That is a big savings.” Hank glanced over at Bill. He seemed impressed.

Stanton continued. “We're always looking for ways to eliminate tangibles. It's the green wave of the future, I'm sure you agree. Everything you see in my office was made from recycled material. But I'm sure you didn't come here to hear me rave about New Age Banking.”

"Well, no. We're investigating the assaults on those women you probably heard about on the news.” Bill pulled out his notepad.

"The ones who had their thumbs cut off?”

"Yes, we were hoping you might know something about that.”

"I don't understand."

"All five of those women do business with your bank."

"Oh, no! I prayed this wouldn't happen." Stanton seemed mortified.

"You act as though you expected this."

"I did. It was a running joke among those in my research and development group. I even voiced my concerns to the board of directors. Of course, they turned a deaf ear when they considered the profitability of eliminating the need for plastic cards. Gentlemen, I am truly sorry."

* * *

The detectives hung back, waiting for the SWAT officer to ram the door. Once it was battered open, the team stormed the apartment.

After a thorough search, an officer shouted, "All clear!"

A young man kneeled in the middle of the living room, hands on the top of his head.

Hank walked up to the suspect. "Are you Thomas Meyers?"

"Yeah."

"Are you currently employed at New Age Bank's Research and Development Department?"

"What's this all about?"

"You're under arrest for aggravated assault, robbery, identity theft, and bank fraud." Hank grabbed Meyers by the hand, then held it behind his back to slip on the cuffs.

He did the same with the other hand.

Bill sauntered into the kitchen. He opened the freezer door. Five human thumbs stood upright in an ice tray. Each thumb was labeled with the victim's name and personal identification number.

Hank peered into the freezer. "Looks like the New Age Bank ATM Thumbprint Recognition Program might have a few bugs."

***

A couple days later, a woman was viciously killed at a different bank's ATM, her face brutally slashed to ribbons, her right eye scooped out of its socket.

The detectives headed over to interview the bank manager. On the way up the elevator, Hank sighed. "Do you think these guys even considered the ramifications of installing retina scanners in their ATMs?"

Bill shrugged. "Here we go again."

8
CASE NUMBER: 18-04-243

Hank watched the woman as she intently studied the photograph.

"No, that's not him."

"You're sure?"

"Positive."

"Okay. What about this one?" Hank replaced the photo with another one.

The woman shook her head right away. "The guy's face was fatter."

"Maybe you should take another look." Bill sat to the right of the woman. Hank faced her on the left.

They had been flipping photos for her for almost an hour. She'd shaken her head at nearly a hundred mugshots.

Instead of overwhelming her with the thick volumes of repeat offenders, twenty per page, the detectives showed her one picture at a time, a technique professed to guarantee better results. The witness would concentrate on the single image without the distraction or influence of surrounding photographs.

"I told you before, it's *not him*!" The woman batted the photo across the table.

Hank snatched up the photograph. "Okay, last one." He placed the final headshot on the table.

"That's him!"

Normally, the detectives would have been ecstatic.

"You're sure?" Bill pushed the photo closer to the woman.

"Yes, I'm sure. He's the man I saw strangle that poor woman in the supermarket parking lot."

"That's the guy?" Hank sighed.

"What *is* it with you two? Don't you understand English? I know what I saw. It's him!"

"Very well. You may go. We'll be in touch." Bill scooted his chair away from the table.

The woman stood up, slowly rubbing the small of her back. Her eyes were puffy from staring at the photographs.

Hank helped her with her coat. "We appreciate you coming in."

The woman grumbled something under her breath. She grabbed her purse, mumbling as she shuffled out of the squad room.

"Jenkins! Hendrix!" boomed a thunderous voice.

"Oh, jeez." Hank cringed.

The captain stepped out of his office. He headed straight for the detectives.

"So, did she ID him?" He chomped on the donut in his hand, nearly devouring it in one bite. He was a robust man, six-foot-three, barrel-chested, with a bit of a gut. He always seemed to have a stain somewhere on his crinkled white shirt, which, more often than not, was a fruity spot from a leaky, jelly-filled donut.

Bill fidgeted in his chair. "Not exactly."

The captain licked his sticky fingers. He picked the photograph up from the table. "Don't tell me." The captain stared at the picture taken of him six months ago for a departmental newsletter. "She chose me."

In a real lineup, it was a common practice to include cops in street clothes as stand-ins, shoulder-to-shoulder alongside the real suspects, facing the one-way mirror. The witness usually lost credibility whenever a cop was picked out as the accused.

In the same light, it was not uncommon to sneak in a few pictures of law enforcement, adding them to the mix to test the witness when going through mug shots, knowing that, if an officer was chosen, the person in question would immediately be disregarded, and the witness would be excused.

"Afraid so." Hank crossed his arms, leaning back in his swivel chair.

"Maybe your eyewitness needs glasses." The captain slurped the last of the gooey filling out of his pastry and popped the rest into his mouth.

"She seemed pretty certain." Bill wearily shook his head.

"Looks like you boys are back to square one. Stay on top of it." The captain marched back into his office.

* * *

IN CASE OF CARNAGE

Two days later, the killer struck again.

This time, the victim was strangled while waiting on the bench for the last scheduled bus just before midnight, not far from where the first victim was slain.

The only person who witnessed the heinous crime unfold was a city bus driver who had pulled up to the passenger loading stop. No one else was aboard the bus at the time to corroborate his story.

The detectives waited at their desks for the eyewitness to show up. Bill kicked back in his chair and shuffled the photographs like a deck of cards, his feet up on his desk, while Hank impatiently tapped his pencil on the side of his empty coffee cup.

Hank glanced over Bill's shoulder. He waved his hand to get his partner's attention. "Here comes the captain."

Bill swung his feet off the desk and sat up straight.

The captain paused at their desks a moment to pull on his overcoat. "I'm on my way over to the mayor's office to do some damage control. He's afraid we may have a serial killer terrorizing the city. I'm inclined to agree. Last thing we need is a citywide panic on our hands. You boys keep me posted. Let me know if you have better luck with the bus driver."

"Yes, sir," Hank replied.

"We're on it," Bill assured his superior.

"Better be, or this could get ugly." The captain stomped out of the squad room.

Ten minutes later, the bus driver arrived.

The detectives listened to the man's story, then made him retell it, in case he thought of something important he might have forgotten. They showed him the photographs of the suspects one at a time.

Fifteen minutes in, the bus driver stabbed the single photo on the desk with the tip of his finger. "That's the creep!"

The detectives glanced at the photograph, taking a moment to look at each other.

Hank picked up the photo. "That's the man you saw strangling the woman at the bus stop?"

"That's right! I'm sure of it!" The bus driver gave Hank a firm nod.

"There isn't any question in your mind? I mean, it was dark." Bill played along as devil's advocate.

"Believe me, that's one face you never forget."

"Yeah, I'm beginning to agree." Hank placed the picture back on the table.

"So, can I go? I really need to get back to the terminal." The bus driver grabbed the armrests on his chair, ready to propel to his feet.

Bill waved his hand dismissively. "You can go."

The bus driver sprang out of his chair and scurried for the exit.

"This is getting a little too weird."

"I'll say." Hank stuffed the photo back in the deck. "That's the second eyewitness to pick the captain's picture."

They returned to their desks, which faced each other.

"You don't think it could possibly be the captain?" Bill pondered.

"No way."

"Then he must have a doppelganger."

"A what?"

IN CASE OF CARNAGE

"A doppelganger. Someone who closely resembles the captain. Did you know there's someone out there in the world who looks exactly like you—an exact replica? I'm not pulling your leg. I read it somewhere."

"Get out of here. Next you'll be telling me there's a parallel universe out there."

"There have been scientific studies suggesting an alternate universe might—"

"So you're telling me there's a bad captain out there murdering women?" Hank rolled his eyes, shaking his head.

"Who looks exactly like our captain."

"I'm not buying it."

"Did you know the captain has a twin brother?"

"No, I didn't."

"I did some digging. Have his address right here." Bill held up a slip of paper.

"We should pay him a visit." Hank grabbed his jacket off the back of his chair as they raced out of the squad room.

***

Hank and Bill sat on a plush leather sofa in an ornate home office, one wall clustered with framed medical degrees and lifetime achievements.

The man in the wheelchair was the spitting image of the captain, except for the full cast on his right leg. "That'll teach me to look both ways."

"So, you were run over coming out of the hospital where you work?" Hank sat forward on the couch, taking notes.

"That's right. As soon as I stepped off the curb. Never even stopped. Fractured my leg in three places."

"And you have no idea who the driver was?"

"No, it happened too fast."

"I guess we have no more questions, doctor. Thank you for your time." Hank closed up his pad.

The detectives stood and headed for the door.

"Tell my brother I'd appreciate if he caught whoever ran me over."

Hank turned to the doctor. "One more question. Do you mind telling us where you two were born? What hospital?"

"Saint Vincent Memorial. I believe they converted it to a small community clinic for the destitute. Why do you ask?"

"It's for our report."

Bill waited until they were outside walking to their car before saying, "I guess that rules out the brother."

"Maybe. Maybe not."

* * *

"Watch your step. I apologize for the mess." The elderly clerk gripped the rickety handrail as he led the detectives to the basement. A thick film of dust covered hundreds of cardboard boxes that were shoved onto storage shelves with more containers stacked on the concrete floor.

Bill gazed at the mountain of boxes. "Sure you can find the file in all this?"

"It may look chaotic, but I have a system." The archivist pressed a bony finger to his lips, scanning the boxes of medical records. He shuffled over to a short stack of boxes under the basement window.

He removed the lid from the top box.

A few seconds later, he handed Hank a medical folder. "Hope you find what you're looking for. Let me know if you need anything else." The clerk climbed back up the stairs.

Hank opened the medical file and studied the front page. "I thought as much." He handed the folder to Bill.

"Triplets? There's a third brother?"

"I don't know. Says here he died at birth."

Bill fanned through the rest of the six-page file. "So where's the death certificate?"

* * *

The next night, Hank and Bill staked out the supermarket parking lot, while the captain kept an eye on the killer's recent bus stop.

A female officer acted as a decoy, her yoga pants flared just enough to hide the weapon strapped to her ankle. She stood by the bench, pretending to wait for the next bus, keeping the detectives posted with a hidden microphone.

It didn't take long before she whispered, "He's right behind me."

Hank and Bill sprang from their car when they heard her scream. Crossing the parking lot, they saw the captain standing in the middle of the street, the female officer lying nearby on the sidewalk.

The detectives heard the rumble of an approaching vehicle. A speeding city bus barreled down the street. The bright headlights showcased the captain as he splattered onto the front grill, the transit bus screeching to a complete stop.

The side door folded open. The driver bounced down the steps—the same man who'd been to the police station. "I nailed the sucker! I got the killer!"

"You killed our captain, you idiot!" Bill grabbed the driver and wrestled him to the ground. He snapped on the cuffs.

"My God!" Hank stared at the mangled lump of human flesh heaped in front of the bus.

"Release him!" a voice bellowed.

The detectives turned. They saw the captain bending to help the female officer to her feet.

Bill couldn't believe it. "You're alive!"

"Of *course* I'm alive. What? You thought that was *me* in the street?"

* * *

Hank and Bill celebrated closing the doppelganger case the next day by bringing the captain a baker's dozen of his favorites from Heavenly Donuts.

Later that evening, the night janitor made his rounds cleaning the squad room. He flipped on the office lights and spotted the pink box on the captain's desk. His mouth watered as he picked up the trash bin and dumped the crumpled papers into the black plastic bag hanging on his cart, his eyes never wavering from the tempting box. He went around, dusting crumbs from the captain's desktop and chair. The impulse became too much. He raised the lid and saw thirteen donuts still in the box. "Who even does that? That's sick."

Each donut had one large bite out of it.

9
CASE NUMBER:
18-04-244

"That guy over there keeps staring at us," Sharon observed.

"Who?" Crandall paused before taking another bite out of his fist-sized burrito.

They nibbled their lunch at a small table in the middle of the mall's food court, surrounded by fifty or more other people.

Sharon stared at the tabletop, twirling the plastic fork's tines in her fried noodles. "Behind you, three tables away."

Crandall began to turn in his seat.

"*Don't*," Sharon hissed, peering over Crandall's shoulder. "He's still checking us out."

"What does he look like?"

"Short hair, dark blue jacket, black T-shirt, jeans."

"Is he still watching us?"

"Okay. He just turned away."

Crandall glanced over his shoulder.

"Ever seen him before?"

"He doesn't look familiar." Crandall dumped his half-eaten burrito into the bag. He grabbed Sharon's tray. "Let's go."

Sharon grabbed her shopping bag next to her chair. Crandall stopped briefly, tilting the swinging door of a trash bin and dumping their uneaten food inside before setting the tray on top. They strode out of the food court, walking briskly between the second-floor shops.

Sharon paused near the entrance to a clothing store. To give Randall an opportunity to sneak a peek down the corridor, she pretended to rummage through the bag she was carrying, which was full of items purchased at a thrift store earlier.

"He's over at the Payless pretending to look at shoes," Crandall whispered.

"What should we do?"

"I say we get the hell out of here." Crandall led the way to the escalator, and they scurried down. As soon as they reached the ground floor, they scuttled for the nearest exit.

Crandall pushed the bar, shoving open the glass door that led outside. The couple bolted down the sidewalk and dashed out onto the parking lot as if they were being pursued by a raging tsunami.

Their Buick was only a row away.

Sharon glanced over her shoulder. "Here he comes!"

Crandall had already reached the driver door and slid behind the steering wheel. He slammed his door just as Sharon reached the locked passenger door. She pounded on the window, yelling his name.

He started the engine and unlocked the passenger door. Sharon flung open her door and dove into the car.

Crandall jammed the gearshift into reverse and lurched out of the parking space. He stomped on the gas, rocketing the Buick between the cars.

He glanced in the rearview mirror. Their pursuer raced toward a pickup truck. Crandall leaned on the wheel, hanging a hard right, steering the Buick toward the nearest exit ramp. Ahead, the traffic light changed from green to yellow, but he gunned the engine, and they blasted through the red light.

After traveling a few miles, they got snarled in traffic, forcing Crandall to slow down. Sharon peered out the rear window to see if they were being followed.

"Did we lose him?" Crandall asked.

"I think so," Sharon responded, straining to see past the cars behind them.

"I'd better keep driving around just to be sure."

***

At nightfall, they pulled up the narrow driveway and parked underneath the sagging carport that was attached to the small rundown house. Concrete steps led to the screened-in front porch. A waist-high chain-link fence guarded a dead patch of lawn.

They entered the side door. Sharon flicked on the light. The kitchen stunk from takeout containers left on the kitchen counter and the sink full of dirty dishes.

Sharon looked around the room, twitching like a pigeon on a food hunt. "We should pack up."

"What, now?"

"Yes, right now."

"We're paid up to the end of the month."

"I don't care. It's not safe."

"How about we give it another day or two?" Crandall lit up a smoke. "Then, if you still want, we'll leave."

"Why? So you can have your little fun?"

"You get off on it just as much as I do."

Suddenly, the room went pitch dark.

"What the hell happened to the lights?"

"I'll bet it's a damn fuse." Crandall thumbed his cigarette lighter, following the flickering glow to a door. "I'll be right back." He unlocked the two dead bolts. He opened the door and descended the stairs into the gloomy basement.

Sharon fumbled around in the dark, opening drawers, feeling inside, until her fingers closed around a book of matches and a used candle. She struck a match and lit the wick on the short, waxy nub. The tenebrous room brightened slightly.

Somewhere in the house, a window shattered.

"Crandall! Get up here!" She reached into her purse and retrieved a small handgun.

The intruder stepped brazenly into the kitchen.

"Who are you?" Sharon shouted, raising the gun. "What do you want?"

Before she could pull the trigger, the man wrenched the gun from her, snapping her fingers like icicles. He gripped her by the throat, crushing her windpipe. She slumped to the floor.

Crandall came up the stairs and stepped into the

kitchen. "Strange. It wasn't the fuse. Must be the—"

The man shot Crandall dead center in the chest.

Crandall stumbled backwards into the open basement door, knocking it shut. He fell back against the wall and collapsed to the floor.

The shooter slumped into a kitchen chair. He stared at his cell phone for a long time before placing the call.

* * *

The detectives arrived to find the suspect in handcuffs. Officer Silverman stood next to the man, who was seated at the table. He eagerly relayed his report. "This is Jeremy Lambert. He confesses to illegally entering the premises, strangling the woman, then shooting the man. Afterward, he dialed 9-1-1 to turn himself in."

Hank looked down at Lambert. "So why'd you do it?"

"They murdered my sister."

Bill took out his notepad. "What's your sister's name?"

"Susan. Susan Lambert."

"And when was this?"

"Three months ago." Lambert lowered his head. "They grabbed her in a parking garage. Cameras got the whole thing. Cops traced the license plate to a remote cabin." He glared at the two bodies on the floor. "By the time they got there, these two were long gone."

"What about your sister?"

"I don't know. They never found her body."

"So how did you find them?"

"When the cops stopped calling me, I hired a private investigator. The guy bled me dry, but he finally tracked them down. I took over from there.”

Bill crossed his arms. “How do we know you’re not feeding us a story?”

“Did you guys hear something?” Officer Silverman asked.

“Hear what?” Bill asked.

The young officer stepped around the dead man on the floor. He opened the door leading down into the basement. “I think it was coming from down there.”

Lambert sat up straight in his chair.

“I’ll go check it out.” Hank started down, the boards creaking underfoot with every step. Cobwebs hung from the dank ceiling at the bottom of the stairwell. The oubliette cellar smelled of mold. He brushed the wall with his fingertips until he found the light switch. He flipped it on.

A doe-eyed creature stared up at him from a grungy mattress tucked against the cinderblock wall on the damp cement floor. Shackled to a pipe, the bruised woman wore a filthy T-shirt that was too large for her emaciated frame, her hair a scraggly bird’s nest. A dirty strip of tape covered her mouth.

Hank knelt beside her. He removed the adhesive slowly. “Don’t be afraid. I’m a cop. What’s your name?”

Her lips trembled. “Susan.”

“Oh my God, is your brother in for a *big* surprise.”

10
CASE NUMBER:
18-05-245

Hank and Bill stepped gingerly into the dark back alley, careful not to tread on the gory viscera from the mutilated body.

Hank shook his head. "This makes the fourth one in the past four months."

"I'm telling you, it's the work of a werewolf."

"Will you stop, Bill? There's no such thing."

"Then why does it only strike when the moon is full?"

"I don't know."

Bill averted his eyes from a coil of intestines that were entwined like a bed of pink snakes. Instead, he gazed at the alleyway, which looked as though a kindly butcher had chucked out scraps to feed a sorry lot of starving mongrels. He spotted a ravaged section of thigh on the ground. Pronounced bite marks surrounded the crater of missing flesh. "So why do you think the lab keeps finding traces of canine saliva on the attack victims?"

"Probably left behind by dogs when they tried to walk off with the evidence."

"Only these aren't your run-of-the-mill mutts we're dealing with." Bill reached into his jacket. He removed a speedloader from his belt. He offered the circular clip of .38 projectiles to Hank.

"I already have ammo."

"Take them. They're silver. You're going to need them if we come up against a werewolf."

Hank held up his hand, refusing the speedloader. "I'll take my chances."

* * *

Jon leaped onto the rear porch.

He tapped the unlit bulb over the back door. Earlier, he'd unscrewed it enough so it wouldn't turn on—a trick to make Cynthia think the filament had blown. He knew she would ask him to replace the bulb. She often made simple requests of him, little handyman jobs to perform around her house—along with his *other* services.

He opened the back door and crept into the house.

Moonlight shimmered through the bedroom door-way and into the dark hallway.

He stepped over the discarded clothes on the floor.

Cynthia lay sound asleep in bed.

Jon snuck into the bathroom. He closed the door ever so quietly and turned on the light. He admired his naked form in the vanity mirror, his muscular body sheening from jogging in the mist, his flesh speckled from head to toe with blood.

In the billowing steam, the scalding shower spray skimmed away the smirch, the incriminating grunge swirling down the drain. Jon lathered his body. He shampooed his thick mane. Rinsing off, he imagined himself in the wild, standing under a waterfall.

After drying himself, he crawled naked into bed next to Cynthia. She moaned, emerging from a deep sleep. She opened one eye. "Where *were* you?" she cooed.

"Feeding the fish." He kissed the tip of her delicious nose.

"If I had a key, I could have come over."

"I didn't want to bother you."

"I'm only next door, silly," Cynthia whispered, gazing into his amber eyes.

Jon reached under the covers.

Cynthia squirmed with delight. "So, you *do* love me."

"Go back to sleep."

Cynthia mewled, closing her eye. She nestled her head on his hairy chest.

Jon stared at the moon through the bedroom window.

The moon grinned back.

* * *

For two hours, the detectives canvassed the neighboring buildings, knocking on doors. Hoping to maximize their chances of locating at least one credible witness, they'd split up to question the residents.

Only a few people had heard the screams. Hardly anyone had bothered to go to the window, caring less what happened to a complete stranger. Those interviewed had been rude, complaining about being rousted out of bed at such an ungodly hour.

The detectives met back at their car to compare notes.

Hank consulted his notepad. "I found the woman who made the call. She swears she saw a large animal charging through the alley on all fours. So I *am* right. It *is* a dog!"

"I have a guy claims he saw a naked man run out after he heard the screams."

"He was probably half asleep."

Bill whipped a bill out of his wallet. "Ten bucks it's a werewolf."

"You're on. Be the easiest ten bucks I ever won."

***

A month later, Bill stood in the squad room, staring out the office window at the full moon. Hank returned from the break room, carrying two steaming cups of coffee. He placed Bill's mug on his desktop blotter before sitting at his own desk.

Officer Silverman rushed in. "Did you hear what happened?"

"No, what?" Hank swiveled in his chair to keep pace with the young man, who was flying by like a clay bird at a gun range.

"Someone robbed the truck before it could make its delivery to our armory."

"What'd they get?"

Hustling out of the room, the recruit yelled over his shoulder, "They haven't posted it yet! The captain's fit to be tied!"

Bill continued to stare out the window. "Did you know lunacy is thought to be related to phases of the moon?"

"I believe it." Hank got up from his desk. He went over to the city street map thumbtacked to the wall.

"The press doesn't believe these are animal attacks. They're calling him 'The Lunar Killer.'"

"They don't watch out, they're going to set off a city-wide panic." Hank studied the five pushpins on the city map. "Hey, Bill. Take a look at this."

Bill stepped across the room.

"Let's see what happens when I connect the murder sites." Hank drew lines from one pushpin to another with a black marker pen. The star shape looked like a pentagram a satanic cult might paint on a floor and surround with candles for a ritual sacrifice.

Bill took a closer look. "That's a little freaky."

"I'll bet my pension"—Hank stabbed the center of the star with the pen tip—"they're hiding here in some abandoned building."

"Werewolves *are* territorial."

"So is a dog pack." Hank grabbed his coat off the back of his chair. "Come on. Let's go scout the area."

* * *

As the Highland District was near the center of the pentagram, they drove through the depressed area of abandoned warehouses and aging brownstone tenements—the ideal breeding ground for night marauders.

Bill stared tentatively over the top of the steering

wheel, guiding the black sedan down the street like a prowling panther. Hank shined the bright spotlight into an alley as they drove by.

Bill braked at a traffic light.

Hank drew his snub-nosed Smith & Wesson out of his holster. He flipped open the cylinder to check his weapon.

Bill reached into his jacket side pocket. He took out the speedloader of silver bullets. "Put these in."

"Are you nuts?"

"Just humor me, okay?"

"You're being ridiculous."

"Come on. What's it going to hurt?"

"I can't believe I'm doing this." Hank pointed the gun muzzle up and extracted the six semi-jacketed metal point bullets onto the palm of his hand. He stuffed the loose cartridges into his coat pocket. He took the speed-loader from Bill and shoved the silver bullets into the cylinder.

The light turned green and Bill accelerated. "You'll be thanking me later."

Hank holstered his gun. "Whatever."

*   *   *

Jon ran naked through the grassy yard. He vaulted over a picket fence and landed on the sidewalk, his bare feet slapping the pavement. Keeping to the shadows, he jogged down a side street with the powerful grace of an antelope loping on the savanna.

He glanced down at a stand of water, catching a

glimpse of the beast before splashing through.

He picked up a scent and came to a crashing halt. His chest heaved from exertion, though he was far from exhausted. A supercharged rush of adrenaline coursed through his body, enhancing the thrill of the hunt.

His ears perked up at the sound of light foot-steps approaching.

He sprang into the nearest alleyway to hide.

* * *

Bill turned the corner onto a dimly lit street. Hank spotted a woman walking half a block away. "You'd better pull over."

"I don't know, Hank. Last time we gave someone a lift, it didn't turn out so great."

The woman was suddenly yanked off her feet into an alley.

Bill slammed on the brakes. "Did you see that?"

"Hit the horn!" Hank sprang from the car, drawing his weapon.

Bill sounded the car horn in an attempt to disrupt the attacker, hopefully giving Hank the precious seconds he needed to save the woman from a savage death.

Hank darted around the corner of the building.

Bill got out and raced after him.

The woman screamed. A single gunshot sounded.

Coming upon the alley's entrance, Bill slipped. He went down like a baseball player sliding into home plate as a massive shape leaped over him.

"Bill, you okay?" Hank stepped out of the alleyway.

IN CASE OF CARNAGE

"What the hell *was* that thing?"
"I don't know. Come on, before it gets away."
"What about the woman?"
"I was too late."

* * *

Cynthia opened the cabinet under the sink. She pulled the bulging garbage sack out of the plastic refuse bin, then carried it out the back door. A full moon shone brightly in the night sky, casting a bluish glow over the backyard.

She walked to the side of the house where she kept the trash can.

A deep growl rumbled from the next yard on.

"Jon? Is that you?" She dropped the bag into the can and replaced the lid.

A cloud shrouded the moon, blanketing the yard in darkness.

She heard stealthy footsteps in the other yard. "Would you like to come over? My porch light seems to have gone out."

The beast leaped over the fence, knocking Cynthia to the ground.

Cynthia let out a bloodcurdling scream.

Gleaming white fangs silenced her when they sank into her slender neck. Sharp teeth tore at her clothes, ripping her face and chest.

* * *

"Did you hear that?" Hank yelled over his shoulder, running a few steps ahead of Bill.

"Came from behind that house."

The detectives darted between two single-story ranch homes and raced down the picket fencing that separated the backyards.

Hank slowed to a walk. He peered into the next yard. "Jesus, he got another one."

Bill hopped over the fence. His shoes squished down on the soggy turf, which had pooled with blood. He looked at the woman who was sprawled on the grass, her face mauled beyond recognition, her throat flayed like a gutted fish.

A hinge screeched. Hank spun around, spotting a naked man darting into the back door of the house. "It's him!" Hank bolted for the back porch.

"Wait up!" Bill shouted.

Hank was already up the steps, entering the house.

Bill jumped over the fence. He caught a glimpse of the steely moon making a break from the imprisoning cloud cover.

Hank crept through the kitchen, clutching his gun in a two-handed grip. Pausing at the threshold, he peered into the gloomy parlor.

A hand gripped his shoulder.

"It's me," Bill whispered.

A tattered armchair and swayback sofa furnished the room. On a wooden stand, a large aquatic tank glowed through algae-covered glass, dead fish floating belly-up on the murky surface.

Bill followed Hank down the hallway.

IN CASE OF CARNAGE

They stopped at the first door.

Hank positioned himself on one side of the door-jamb, Bill on the other.

Bill turned the knob, easing the door open to a bedroom devoid of furniture. The closet door gaped open—empty.

They continued down the hall to a grungy bathroom with soiled towels all over the floor and a plastic shower curtain draped halfway across the tub.

Hank kept his gun pointed at the tub and snapped the curtain open.

A rusty waterline rimmed the pitted porcelain. Globs of black hair clogged the drain.

They approached the last door at the end of the hall.

Bill pressed his ear to the door. "I hear something." He raised his hand, three fingers extended. He counted off silently, lowering one finger, then another. When the last finger curled down, Hank kicked in the door.

An overwhelming zoo-like ammonia stench, accompanied by the rank odor of aged feces, assaulted their nostrils.

"What the hell died in here?" Stepping into the room, Bill covered his nose and mouth.

The door swung closed, smacking Hank square in the face. He stumbled into the hall. Inside the room, a ferocious growl preceded a crash against the door and Bill's muffled yells.

"Bill, get away from the door!" Hank fired two quick shots into the door. He heard a wounded animal howl, its body thrashing against the floor and walls.

The raucous noise faded to a dead silence.

Hank turned the knob, nudging the door open with the toe of his shoe. He stuck his head in to peek.

Bill crouched between a nightstand with a lamp and the wall.

"Are you okay?" Hank whispered, scurrying over to his partner. He could see Bill's shredded coat sleeve, his exposed arm raked with deep gashes.

"Turned my arm into a damn chew toy." Bill loosened his necktie, slipping it over his head. He shoved the loop up his injured arm and cinched it tight around his bicep as a tourniquet.

The opposite side of the room was pitch-black.

Hank aimed his gun across the bedroom, though he couldn't see a target. "Where is he?"

"It's over there, hiding in the dark."

"Get ready." Hank turned on the lamp.

The low-watt bulb under the thick shade did little to brighten the room.

But it was enough to see the shape hulking in the shadows.

"Go away," spoke a baritone voice.

"Police! Let's see those hands!" Hank pointed his gun.

The naked man stood six feet tall, with thick, shoulder-length black hair. All of his body, except his face, was covered with a dark mat of short, curly hair.

He hunched his shoulders, shifting his weight on his muscular legs like a wrestler challenging an opponent. In a bestial display of rage, he inflated his chest, letting out an ear-piercing, wolf-like howl that was so loud, it reverberated off the walls.

The naked man charged across the room.

IN CASE OF CARNAGE

Hank and Bill fired their revolvers. The room boomed with gunfire, fiery gases blazing out of both barrels in a smoky haze.

The naked man flailed, bullets riddling his chest, one slug exploding his right eye, another punching a hole into his forehead. He toppled backwards, landing spread-eagle on the hardwood floor.

Hank stood and helped Bill to his feet.

"Good thing we used silver bullets." Bill loosened the necktie around his arm so as not to cut off the circulation.

"The guy's no more a werewolf than I am." Hank opened the bail on his snub-nosed .38. He ejected the empty casings onto the floor. Then he grabbed a speed-loader from his jacket pocket and put fresh bullets in.

"Well, he *was* until he changed. How do you explain what he did to my arm?"

Hank looked down at the dead man. He didn't see any fangs and the man's fingernails were too short to have inflicted Bill's wounds. "There's no way he could have done that to your arm."

"That's because he attacked me when he was a werewolf, before he shapeshifted back."

"Yeah, well that's a load of—"

A rumbling growl came from behind the closed closet door.

"Did you hear that?" Bill holstered his handgun, knowing it would be too difficult to reload one-handed. He reached down and grabbed his backup piece from his ankle holster.

The closet door exploded off the hinges with a loud crash.

A four-legged creature stood on top of the fallen door, glaring at them with cold, beady eyes. The quadruped was black as night, its body thick as a bull's. Large flap ears hung on its massive head, its nostrils flaring on an enormous canine snout. A thin trail of blood ran down its dark fur from the bullet wound in its shoulder.

The beast's slobbery upper lip curled, baring its fierce fangs. Foamy drool pooled onto the floor next to the dead man's right hand.

"What the hell *is* it?"

Hank raised his gun. "It looks like one of those bull mastiff breeds. Look at the size of that thing. It's got to be over two hundred pounds."

"See? I told you it was a dog."

"Yeah, with a lunatic owner."

The monstrous dog lunged.

The detectives opened fire, striking the beast in the face and chest, the bullets seemingly having no effect, until the massive creature crashed dead on the floor, mere inches away from their feet.

Hank draped Bill's arm over his shoulder and helped his partner to the door. "Let's get you stitched up."

"Still want that ten bucks?"

"Keep it. Maybe this'll teach you there're no such things as werewolves."

"Had you believing it."

"Shut up and quit bleeding all over the place."

11
CASE NUMBER: 18-06-246

Pelting rain ricocheted off the metal rooftop of the unmarked sedan like a spray of bullets at a gun range.

"Hell, it's like driving under Niagara Falls," Bill griped, squinting over the steering wheel. "I can't see a damn thing."

Even on the fastest setting, the wipers did little to improve visibility, swiping from side to side like a pair of frantic metronomes, the headlight beams swallowed up in the deluge.

Hank squinted out the side window. "It's not much farther."

Bill pulled up to the curb.

The downhill intersection was impassable. Two cars were abandoned in the middle of the street, the waterline up to the door handles.

"What now?"

"Better put on your waders." Hank pulled his poncho

hood over his head and climbed out of the car.

Bill turned off the engine. He zipped up his raincoat and stepped into the torrential rain.

The detectives braved the storm, trudging down the sidewalk.

A sudden gale nearly blew them off their feet.

They forged on until they reached an alleyway leading into a box canyon of warehouses. The rooftop runoff cascaded down the steep walls, splashing through the fire escape ironwork.

Hank and Bill waited under a loading dock overhang.

"I can't believe we're out in this." Bill shook his shoulders to propel the water off his raincoat.

"The storm should give us the element of surprise."

"Sure hope so. This tip of Dunks's better pan out."

"He's *your* snitch."

"I know, Hank. I'm just saying."

"He's been a reliable source so far. If he says he knows where we can find this Vorlock character, I'm inclined to believe him."

"Hank Jenkins, always the optimist."

"Well, it's that, or we're out here taking a shower for nothing."

"This guy's pretty ballsy, robbing a blood bank."

"Human blood's a lucrative business on the black market."

"Especially if you're a vampire."

"What, like the ones at the mall? Don't even *go* there."

"Go where?" Bill gave Hank a smirk.

"Will you can it with the vampire crap?"

"You got a better explanation?"

"Let's be logical. Vorlock is just another illegal trafficker out to make a quick buck. He saw the Red Cross as an easy mark."

"Or he got tired of going out to hunt and decided to stockpile for the winter."

"Give it a rest. There are heists happening everywhere. Even *we* got hit."

"Yeah, the captain is still champing at the bit. He was looking forward to getting his hands on those upgraded Glock automatics and those new bulletproof vests."

"Enough gabbing. Let's go." Hank stepped into the rain, Bill on his heels.

They sprinted twenty yards before ducking into an alcove outside an apartment lobby. A notice posted on the glass declared the property condemned with a scheduled date for demolition. The latch bolt had been sheared off, either from a previous break-in or by the demolition team prepping the site.

Hank pushed through the door into a small entryway with marred flooring, black, dried adhesive squares where tiles used to be. Rival gang insignias tagged the walls. Dark-colored rectangles haunted the chipped paint where pictures once hung. The ingress was devoid of any furniture.

Key-access mailboxes grouped together on the wall, most of the small doors either open or ripped off their tiny hinges. Nearly every resident nametag was gone.

An upside-down smiley face sticker and "C. Vorlock" labeled the metal front of one mailbox.

"I wonder what the 'C' stands for," Hank said.

Bill studied the mailbox. "Oh, I don't know. Maybe 'Count'?"

"Will you put a sock in it?"

"You don't have to get all testy."

Hank glanced around. "It's just like Dunks described it. You brought the warrant, right?"

"No, I thought *you* did."

"Aw, man!"

"Yeah, I got it." Bill patted his raincoat side pocket to reassure Hank.

"One of these days, Alice . . ." Hank said, doing his Jackie Gleason bit.

"I hope you're up for a barbecue."

"Barbecue?"

"Yeah, I brought the stakes."

"What are you babbling about?"

Bill unzipped his rain slicker. He showed Hank the two sharpened wooden stakes tucked inside his belt.

"You're certifiable, you know that?"

"Scoff all you like, buddy boy! But don't come crying to me when Vorlock's taking a bite out of your neck."

"Don't worry. I won't."

"Think this 'Vorlock' has a crew with him?"

"Why? You think we need backup?" Hank glanced out the front window. The rain pelted so hard, he could barely see the other side of the street. "It'd take them forever to get here in this weather."

"Hey, the guy's probably up there passed out anyway." Bill led the way over to the service elevator. The door was open, the car suspended four feet up, apparently stuck due to a mechanical malfunction. "Looks like we're taking the stairs."

"Which floor did Dunks say this guy's on?"

IN CASE OF CARNAGE

Bill gazed up the dark stairwell. "All the way to the top."

The detectives proceeded up the stairs. They found each level littered with trash, either left behind by previous tenants or brought in by homeless squatters: stained mattresses in the hallways, broken bottles, discarded syringes on the floors.

Bill stepped away from the wall to make room for a rat that was scurrying along the baseboard. "Not exactly the Hilton."

When they reached the eighth and final floor, Bill took a second to catch his breath.

"Maybe it's time to cut back on the donuts."

"Maybe it's time to shut your pie hole," Bill shot back.

Hank approached the blue door at the end of the hall. He waited for Bill before pointing to the inverted smiley face sticker affixed above the doorknob. "Like following bread crumbs."

Bill pushed on the door, edging it open. He glanced over at Hank. "This is a little too easy."

The detectives drew their weapons and stepped inside. The huge loft was the size of a basketball court, with thick stanchions throughout supporting the high ceiling. Rain spattered the windows overlooking the nightscape, the heavy drumming on the roof echoing inside the cavernous chamber. A constellation of pillar candles glowed about the large space, resembling a midnight vigil held for a fallen loved one.

Bill walked up to a wall that was plastered with horror movie posters—titles like *Fright Night*, *Nosferatu*, *From Dusk Till Dawn*, *Near Dark*, *The Lost Boys*, *Vampyres*. Famous stars like Bela Lugosi in *Dracula*, Tom Cruise in

Interview with the Vampire.

As a joke, someone had drawn black fangs on Sarah Michelle Gellar, who was posing in a *Buffy the Vampire Slayer* poster.

"What in the world?" Hank inspected a row of pine coffins, which were lined up near the wall with pillows and blankets.

"Looks like we stumbled upon a coven of vampires."

"No, this is crazy."

The detectives entered a lounge area with a large sectional couch and three reclining chairs, all facing a sixty-inch plasma screen with state-of-the-art surround-sound speakers arranged around the home theatre for optimal viewing.

Bill checked out the equipment. "Sweet setup."

Paused on the TV screen was as black-and-white shot of a middle-aged woman with a beehive hairdo who was standing by a man in a tweed jacket. Both were staring up at an oil portrait of a sinister-looking man. The mysterious man on the canvas wore a dark coat with a high, scalloped collar. He sported a large black-stoned ring on the forefinger of his right hand, which clutched the handle of an elegant cane. An impressive medal was pinned on his chest.

Something swooped from the rafters, skimming over their heads.

Hank ducked. "Damn pigeons."

"Sorry, pal. That was a bat."

"No, it wasn't."

"Trust me. It was a bat. I watched it fly over there." Bill pointed to an enclosed addition made entirely of plywood. The crude structure was relatively square, roughly fifteen feet on every side. A thin strip of light emanated from beneath the door.

The detectives crept across the room. Hank eased the door open.

Five vampires sat around a circular table.

The fiends wore dark clothes and capes. They hunched over individual blood bags, slurping through rose-colored straws like thirsty kids greedily sucking from their juice boxes.

A large glass-door refrigerator unit stood in the corner of the room. Inside, red blood bags crammed the rows of shelves with enough blood to stock a small-town hospital.

A pale, voluptuous vampirette in a sheer teddy stretched out on a purple velvet chesterfield.

Bill cleared his throat. "Sorry to bust up snack time. Which one of you is Vorlock?"

The older-looking vampire sucked his bag dry until it collapsed on itself. He faced the detectives. "I am Vorlock!"

Bill pointed at the man's face. "You . . . uh . . . you got something there."

Vorlock stuck out his tongue to explore the outer regions of his mouth and licked a dab of blood from his upper lip.

"You got it." Bill reached into his raincoat and retrieved a folded slip of paper. "We have a warrant for your arrest."

The other four vampires rose from the table. Their chalky-white faces contrasted with their black, slicked-back hair. The bloodsuckers smacked their ruby-red lips.

"Surely you don't think I am afraid of a silly piece of paper." Vorlock laughed.

"Maybe you'd prefer a different wood product." Bill pulled the two stakes out of his raincoat. He handed a stake to Hank.

Vorlock drew his cape over his face. The other vampires cowered, as though the stakes possessed the destructive power to turn them to dust.

Bill swaggered in front of the doorway. "We can do this the easy way, or we can do it the hard way."

"It's entirely up to you," Hank added.

The four vampires looked to Vorlock for guidance.

Vorlock raised his arms, fanning out his cape. He let out a boisterous laugh. The other vampires joined in. The vampirette cackled from the sofa.

"All right, pipe down!" Hank shouted. "Everyone put your hands on your heads! You're all under arrest!"

The vampires continued to laugh.

"Now you're getting on my nerves." Bill pointed his gun at Vorlock.

The elder stopped laughing. He gave his flock a menacing look, like a teacher silencing a rowdy classroom of students.

Everyone quieted down.

The vampires stood shoulder to shoulder in a half circle, Vorlock in the middle, preparing for a showdown.

The vampirette glided from the couch. She assumed a combative pose in her revealing negligee.

"This is your last warning," Bill said.

"What do we do?" Hank whispered. "They're unarmed."

"Doesn't make them any less dangerous."

Two vampires grabbed the table, shoving it to one side to clear a path.

Vorlock threw back his cape. He leaped into the air like a giant bat, arms outstretched, flashing his long talon fingernails.

The detectives fired single shots.

Each bullet punched into Vorlock's chest, the impact halting him in midair like a windshield smashing into an unsuspecting bug, before he landed flat on his feet. He gazed down to inspect the bullet holes in his shirt. He turned to the other vampires. "Don't worry. It only stings for a second."

Bill grabbed Hank by the arm. "Did you see that? He didn't even bleed."

They bolted out of the ill-constructed room. Somehow, by some unearthly power of teleportation, a vampire blocked the door—the only way out of the loft.

Hank glanced at Bill. "How the hell did he do that?"

"He's a vampire! He can do *anything*!"

Hank aimed his revolver at the vampire. "Move away from the door!"

The vampire hissed.

Hank fired.

The vampire grimaced. He glared at the detectives while rubbing a spot on his chest with his slender fingers. "Your guns are useless on us."

Hank looked to his partner. "What now?"

"Hell, *I* don't know."

Vorlock and the other four vampires marched out of their personal blood dispensary. The vampire at the door made number six. The vampirette had slipped from the room.

"You'd better think fast," Hank said. "You're the supposed expert!"

"Well, they don't like crucifixes, definitely hate garlic."

"Forget all that!"

"Then I guess we're going to have to cut off their heads."

"What?"

"Or we can drive stakes through their hearts."

"What if we just shoot them in the head?"

"Works on zombies."

The detectives pointed their guns at the head of the vampire preventing their escape.

"Hey, whoa!" The vampire held up his hands. "Don't shoot!"

Hank cocked back the hammer. "Suddenly you're afraid of our guns?"

"Please, I'm begging you!"

"Careful, Hank. It's trying to trick us."

Behind them came the distinct sound of a shell being ratcheted into the chamber of a shotgun. Hank and Bill turned slowly.

Armed with a sawed-off shotgun, the vampirette stood in front of a table covered with burning candles. The flickering wicks outlined the curved features of her body through her thin nightdress, except for her upper torso, which was wrapped in a short coat. She aimed the twin barrels at the detectives.

Bill shot her directly between the eyes.

She fell back on the table, scattering the burning candles. Her head became a fiery torch as her teddy caught fire. She screamed, withering to the floor, her body engulfed in flames.

Vorlock and the other vampires reached into their capes and drew Glock automatics and Uzi machine guns.

Bill ducked behind a chair as gunfire erupted. "What the hell!"

Hank dove under a table.

Tracer bullets streaked across the gloomy room like laser beams in a *Star Wars* battle scene, riddling the movie posters on the walls.

A vampire marched across the room, his Uzi spitting out nine-millimeter slugs.

Hank aimed low, blowing out his kneecap. The vampire screamed. He staggered back, then fell to the floor.

A vampire jumped up on the table, then shot down through the wood at Hank.

Hank returned fire. His slug burst through the tabletop into the vampire's groin. The vampire howled, tumbling off the table.

Bill ran out from behind the chair and took cover behind a thick support beam. A vampire blasted lead up and down the opposite side of the post. Splintered wood chips sailed past Bill's head. He stuck his gun hand out blindly and fired two quick shots.

One shattered the vampire's collarbone; the other drilled through his throat. Blood gurgled from the vampire's mouth as his legs gave out.

Hank dashed across the room for a better position, only to be caught in a fierce crossfire between Vorlock and the vampire guarding the door.

With nowhere to run, Hank dove into a casket.

Vorlock fired at the soft pine coffin.

Bill noticed Hank's dilemma and shot at Vorlock, forcing the diabolical creature to scurry for safety behind the plywood structure.

The vampire by the loft's front door bounded toward the caskets. He trained his submachine gun on the first casket and fired off a quick burst. He paused at the next coffin, blasted a deadly hail of bullets into the box, and then turned to the next coffin.

Hank bolted upright, shooting the vampire in the windpipe.

A crimson gush spewed out of the tiny opening. The vampire keeled over in the coffin next to Hank.

Another vampire jumped from the shadows and fired at Hank. The force of the bullet grazing Hank's shoulder pushed him back into the casket.

Bill dispatched the vampire with a clean shot to the skull. He rushed over to check on Hank. Vorlock approached from behind and cracked him on the back of the head with the butt of his handgun.

Bill fell to his knees, then slumped facedown onto the floor. Hank stared up from the casket at Vorlock. He raised his gun. Vorlock kicked the weapon out of his hand. The small revolver spun across the floor.

Vorlock unfastened his cape and allowed it to drop to the floor. He removed his shirt, then unstrapped a Kevlar bulletproof vest and tossed it onto a chair. "I was baking in that thing. Must be all that extra padding."

"So it was *you* who stole our shipment."

"Guilty as charged." Vorlock snickered. "You know, these vests really can stop a fifty-caliber slug. I know. We tried."

"I don't get it," Hank said. "What's with the vampire crap?"

"Hey, who doesn't love vampires?"

"So, what, you just sit around all night, watching movies and drinking blood?"

"Pretty much. What can I say? I'm a big *Dark Shadows* fan. How about yourself?"

Hank shook his head.

Vorlock pointed at the big screen, directing Hank's attention to the man in the portrait. "So you never heard of Barnabas Collins?"

"Can't say as I have." Hank attempted to sit up but fell back. "Tell me . . ." he whispered.

Vorlock drew closer. "What? I didn't catch that."

". . . if this . . ."

Vorlock leaned down over the casket. "You're going to have to speak up. I can't understand a word you're saying."

Hank glared up at Vorlock.

". . . HURTS!"

He drove a wooden stake through Vorlock's chest.

A look of alarm came over Vorlock's pasty face. He gasped, clutching the stake with both hands, then collapsed on his back.

Hank sat up in the coffin.

Bill rubbed the back of his head and gazed around at all the bodies. The vampirette had been reduced to a smoldering, charred husk. "Bet she wished she'd skipped this barbecue."

"Yeah, I don't think Vorlock was especially fond of your choice of stakes."

12
CASE NUMBER: 18-06-247

Vic and Rich enjoyed one last cocktail, while Kate and Debbie scoured the living room, carrying empty glasses and dirty paper plates to the kitchen.

"You sure throw one mean party." Vic tipped his tumbler back to polish off his Black Russian. He crunched the ice cubes, savoring the faint taste of the Kahlúa.

"Glad you approve." Rich propped himself against the wet bar. "You okay to drive?" He leaned to one side.

Vic shot out his hand to steady his friend. "You okay to stand?"

"Apparently not." Rich giggled.

"So who were all those people you invited tonight?"

"Our friends, you silly boy."

"Oh, right."

Kate strode into the living room. She slipped on her coat, then handed Vic his jacket. "We should really get going. It's late."

Vic glanced at his wristwatch. "Oh, you're right. It's after midnight."

Debbie came out of the kitchen, wiping her hands with a dish towel. "Thanks, Kate, for helping me clean up."

"No problem. We had a great time."

Vic put on his jacket. He almost laughed when Rich strode over to the front door, trying not to stagger. Rich was always the gracious host, giving the best parties—though he often overindulged, passing out in the bedroom before the revelry was over. Vic was surprised he was still able to stand, let alone walk.

Rich opened the front door. He leaned on the door-knob for support.

Vic could hear the rain outside. As there had been no mention on the evening news weather report, he hadn't thought to bring an umbrella. "Shoot! I'm parked down the street."

Kate looked outside. "I don't mind getting a little wet."

"No point in us *both* getting drenched. You wait here. I'll get the car and pull up in the driveway." Vic turned up his collar. He hesitated for a split second before bolting into the torrential rain. He had to be careful running in his dress shoes, as they had smooth soles. He didn't want to slip and ruin a good pair of slacks.

Vic tried to hurdle over a large puddle at the end of the driveway, but his right shoe landed in six inches of water.

"Damn it." He shielded his eyes from the rain with his hand and charged down the sidewalk, spotting their car. He stood in the street, fumbling with his car keys to open the driver door.

IN CASE OF CARNAGE

A blunt object rammed into the small of his back. "Hand it over!"

Vic froze. *What the hell is this?*

"Hand it over," the stern voice said again—three simple words that sent shivers down Vic's spine.

The keys jingled in Vic's trembling hand.

The keys! I can use them as a weapon to gouge out his eyes!

But that would require the courage to fight back, and right now Vic was scared out of his mind. "You can have my wallet. . . . It's not much . . . but—"

The prodding left his back. Vic felt the cold muzzle press into his neck. "Here, take them!" Vic raised his hand, jiggling the keys.

He heard the menacing click of the hammer cocking.

"Jesus, man! What the hell do you want? I'll give you anything—"

The gunman smacked Vic on the side of the head. Vic fell against the driver door. He felt his wallet yanked from his back pocket. He grabbed the door handle, twisting around as he slumped onto the pavement with his back to the car.

Vic looked up, the rain in his face.

His attacker stood over him, rifling through Vic's wallet. The thug wore a dark, hooded sweatshirt. He held a large revolver in his right hand, big enough to blow Vic's head clear off his shoulders.

Vic cringed, expecting the man to shoot him execution style. Instead, the man glanced over his shoulder.

A dark shape crashed into him.

Vic watched another man tussle with his assailant in

the middle of the street. They rolled about on the wet pavement, fighting for possession of the gun. A desperate hand yanked the hooligan's hood off his head.

Vic knew he should get up, jump into the fray, assist the Good Samaritan who was risking his life for him, but his legs were rubbery like cooked spaghetti.

If he could only muster the nerve, help his rescuer before someone got—

He flinched when the gun went off.

The man in the sweatshirt scrambled to his feet.

The other man remained on the ground.

Oh my God. He killed him!

The man with the gun stared down at Vic.

Interior lights started to come on in the surrounding houses. A neighbor opened his front door, curious about the gunshot.

Vic's attacker threw the hood over his head. He took off running, vanishing into the night.

A woman rushed over to the prone figure in the street. She dropped to her knees, expelling a gut-wrenching wail, then fainted on top of the body.

Another woman appeared. She crouched in front of Vic. "Oh my God, Vic. Are you hurt?"

Vic looked her straight in the face. "Kate?"

* * *

An hour later, the street outside Rich and Debbie's house buzzed with activity. A patrol car parked at each corner, their rooftop emergency lights flashing like beacons in the night. A reporter stood by a media van, interviewing a small group of people milling about in their bathrobes. Vic's car was cordoned off with yellow police tape, and the street was littered with numbered evidence markers.

Inside the house, Vic and Kate sat on the couch across from Hank, who had been assigned the case. Vic held a frozen packet of peas to the side of his head.

Hank started to speak, then turned his head to sneeze into his coat sleeve. "Sorry about that." His voice was scratchy and hoarse. He looked at Vic. "Are you sure you don't want to go to the hospital? You may have a concussion."

"No, I'm fine."

"Honey, are you sure?" Kate laid her hand on Vic's shoulder. "You took quite a wallop."

"I'm okay, really."

Hank sat forward in his chair. "Mr. Williams, I know how upsetting this must be for you, so I'll try to make this brief."

"Sure, anything. Just catch the bastard. I still can't believe Rich is dead."

"So you didn't know your friend was fighting with your assailant?"

"No, it was all a blur."

Officer Silverman came into the room, balancing three steaming coffee mugs on a tray. He set the tray down on the coffee table. "I reheated what was in the coffee pot."

Kate smiled at the officer. "Thank you."

Silverman nodded. He stepped away, occupying a spot on the other side of the room.

Kate looked at Hank. "Any word on how Debbie is doing?"

Hank glanced over his shoulder at Silverman.

"I just got off the phone with the hospital, sir. She's under sedation."

"Keep me posted. I'll want to question her once she wakes up."

"Yes, sir."

Hank turned his attention back to Vic. "So, tell me about the—" Hank paused to pull a handkerchief out of his pocket. He took a moment to blow his nose. "Sorry. Did you get a good look at the man that robbed you?"

"I saw his face."

"Great. Then I'll need you to come down to the station. You can go through our mugshots while everything is still fresh in your mind. I'm sure this guy already has a record."

"I'm afraid I would be wasting everyone's time." Vic tossed the thawed bag of peas onto the coffee table.

"You just told me you got a good look at his face."

"I did."

"I'm a little confused." Hank turned suddenly, coughing into his hand. He reached into his coat pocket and took out a small packet of sanitizing wipes. He took a moment to clean his hands.

Kate clasped her hands together. "Before you ask my husband any more questions, there's something you should know about him."

"Oh?"

"Have you ever heard of prosopagnosia?"

"No, I can't say I have."

"Vic doesn't recognize faces. His condition is often referred to as 'face blindness.'"

"I never heard of such a thing."

"It's true," Vic said. "I've had it since I was a child." Vic took a sip of his coffee. "The only thing I can tell you is he was wearing a dark, hooded sweatshirt. My parents could walk into this room, and I wouldn't recognize them."

"So, does this affliction have anything to do with your eyesight?"

"On the contrary, I have twenty-twenty vision. No, I believe it has to do with a defect in the brain. To tell you the truth, I don't think they really know."

"That is odd. So, what do you . . .? Excuse me." Hank paused to cough. This time it sounded croupier. "I hope I'm not losing my voice. So what do you see when you look at someone's face?"

"I see a person's facial features, I suppose, like everyone else. I just have no idea who they are. If Kate, my own wife, left the room and came back in, I wouldn't even recognize her."

"That is weird."

"It does have its challenges."

"How do you function at work?"

"I can usually recognize my co-workers by their voices, the way they dress, their body types. Plus, they're pretty good at giving me indicators. Name tags help immensely. But if I saw their faces in a newsletter, I wouldn't know who they were."

Hank cleared his throat. "Did the man who attacked you get a good look at you?"

"Yes, when I thought he was going to kill me."

"Meaning he knows what *you* look like."

Kate sucked in a deep breath. "You don't think he'll come after Vic?"

"It's a possibility—especially if he thinks Vic can identify him. He *does* have Vic's wallet, so he knows where you live."

Vic slammed his mug down on the coffee table. "Christ! What do we do?"

"Don't worry. We'll catch this guy. In the meantime, I'd stay vigilant if I were you. Call us if there's a problem." Hank handed Kate his business card, then dabbed his runny nose with his handkerchief.

Kate slipped the card into her coat pocket. "Hope you feel better."

"Yeah, me too. This cold has been a real pain. I miss not being able to go for a jog." Hank hawked up a loose wad of phlegm deep in his chest.

"Try some honey and hot tea. Works wonders for me whenever I'm feeling like I'm coming down with a cold," Kate suggested.

"Thanks. I'll give it a try."

"Maybe you should take a sick day."

"Not with *my* caseload."

Vic stood up from the couch. "So, can we go?"

"Sure. I'd stick around the house. And, whatever you do, don't trust *anyone*!"

* * *

For the days to follow, Vic was an addled wreck.

IN CASE OF CARNAGE

Why had the detective urged him not to trust anyone?

Vic was so paranoid, he hadn't set foot out of the house once since Rich's murder—not even to retrieve the newspaper off the stoop. Every time he peeked between the curtains, someone would drive by or stroll down the sidewalk. Sure, they were probably only his neighbors running errands or taking walks. But to Vic they were all faceless people, meaning any one of them could be the killer.

Vic wanted to stay holed up in his house, but there was Rich's funeral to attend. He wouldn't be able to live with himself if he didn't pay his respects. After all, Rich *had* saved his life—only to lose his own. It was only right.

***

It rained the day of the funeral.

The mourners huddled under their black umbrellas. Rich's coffin was suspended over a freshly dug grave. Vic and Kate sat next to Debbie to offer their condolences.

The dismal weather accentuated the dark mood.

Every so often, Rich glanced over his shoulder. And every time, he caught a stranger's face staring at him. Would the killer be so bold as to show his face at the funeral?

Vic prayed not. Then how would he know?

After the minister finished with his parting words, Debbie led the procession, tossing handfuls of dirt onto Rich's coffin.

Vic grabbed Kate's arm and started dragging her toward their car.

"Vic, what in the world are you doing?"

"We need to get home."

"Don't forget, we're gathering at Debbie's. I made a casserole."

"You'll have to go by yourself. I need to get—"

Before he could say "home," he spotted a sinister figure standing in the rain, wearing a hooded sweatshirt.

Vic bolted for the car.

"Honey! Wait for me!" Kate called after him.

"I can't! Get a ride with someone!" Vic jumped into the car. He started the engine and raced out of the cemetery. He sped past a stop sign, narrowly missing another motorist.

By the time he reached his first traffic light, he'd regained some of his composure.

While he waited for the light to turn green, a truck pulled up alongside him.

The driver was wearing a hooded sweatshirt.

Vic flipped open his glovebox where he'd hidden his Taurus .22 caliber pistol. Ever since the attack, Vic had kept it handy, and he'd decided to leave it in the car for the funeral.

He glanced up.

The man in the truck stared straight ahead.

Vic raised his gun, finger braced on the trigger.

The man drove through the intersection.

Vic lowered his gun. He trembled, knowing he had almost shot the wrong person.

An impatient motorist blasted a horn.

Vic slipped the pistol into his jacket's side pocket. He tromped on the accelerator, gunning the car down the street. He reached up and grabbed the cigarette packet off the visor. The pack was empty. He crumpled it up and threw it on the car seat.

He needed a cigarette *bad.*

Luckily, a liquor store was up ahead.

He pulled into the tiny parking lot, then got out of the car and did a complete three-sixty, checking for anyone suspicious.

Hell, to Vic, *everyone* looked suspicious.

Inside the store, he didn't recognize the man at the register. He'd probably seen him numerous times, as Vic often stopped here. The clerk didn't seem to recognize Vic—or, if he did, he didn't mention it.

"Can I help you?" the clerk asked.

"Give me a carton of generic lights." Vic arranged his money on the counter.

Half a dozen shoppers milled about the store.

The clerk placed the carton of cigarettes on the counter and opened the register to count Vic's change.

Two people argued behind Vic.

"Hand it over!" A man in a hooded sweatshirt snatched a cereal box away from a woman.

"Jesus!" Vic bolted for the automatic doors, abandoning his purchase on the counter. He scrambled to his car and almost hit a station wagon as he pealed out onto the street.

Vic kept checking the rearview mirror as he raced down the road.

A black sedan followed two car lengths behind.

The driver sported a black sweatshirt with the hood casting a shadow over his unrecognizable face.

Vic ran a red light. He made a hard right, nearly clipping a school bus.

He checked the rearview mirror.

The car remained on his tail.

Vic sped up his driveway and parked.

The black sedan stopped at the curb.

Vic sprinted across the front lawn.

A man in a black sweatshirt, sweatpants, and sneakers exited the car.

Vic pulled his gun. He pointed it at the stranger who was coming up the driveway. "Stay away from me!"

The man extended his hand. "Hand it over!"

Vic pulled the trigger.

The man ducked, dropping to one knee. He drew a small revolver from under his sweatshirt, then returned fire, striking Vic in the shoulder.

Vic dropped his gun. He clutched his shoulder and fell onto the grass.

The man walked over to Vic.

A blue car arrived. Kate got out, hesitated at the passenger door, and leaned back in to the driver. "I'll be right back with my casserole."

She gasped when she found a man pointing a gun at her husband, who was on the ground.

The man looked over at Kate. He pulled the hood away from his face.

Vic waved at Kate with his good arm. "He's been stalking me! He killed Rich."

"Vic, have you lost your mind?"

"It's *him*, I tell you!"

"Vic! It's Detective Jenkins!"

"It can't be! I heard his voice! He doesn't sound anything like the detective!"

Hank put away his gun. "That's because I'm over my cold. Even went for a jog this morning. I came by to thank your wife for that remedy of hers."

13
CASE NUMBER: 18-07-248

Clare looked up as the detectives descended the grassy slope to join her at the construction site. Hank held a travel coffee mug. Bill popped the rest of a glazed donut into his mouth, then licked his sticky fingers.

They studied the man wearing a jogging outfit. He lay flat on his back with rebars sticking out of his chest.

Clare gave the detectives the rundown. "I figure time of death somewhere within twenty-four hours. Judging by his position, I'd say he rolled down the hill. There're blades of grass stuck to the bottom of his running shoes, suggesting the lawn may have been wet, causing him to slip and fall."

"Poor sap." Bill stole Hank's coffee to wash down his donut.

"Hey!" Hank objected. He tried to grab for his mug, but Bill polished it off. Hank turned back to Clare. "Find any identification?"

"No, his pockets were clean. Not even a house key."

"That's strange," Hank said.

"We should probably get someone to post signs warning people of the danger so no one else has an accident," Clare advised.

"Good idea," Bill agreed.

"Yeah," Hank said. "I'd hate to see another innocent person get hurt."

* * *

Thirty-six hours earlier . . .

Marcus opened his eyes. A blackbird glided across the gray sky. He wondered, as he often did, why birds could perch, congregating wherever they pleased, and it seemed so natural, but whenever a homeless man slept in a park, folks found the image appalling.

Marcus was only thirty-five years old, but sleeping on the uneven ground had gnarled his spine like a derailed train. Even though the tattered tarp he'd used for a ground cloth had kept him dry, it had proved an insufficient barrier against the damp chill that had seeped into his weary bones.

He peered through a leafless patch of brush serving as a moderate windbreak. Mallards drifted on a pond in the man-made park of manicured lawns and jogging trails snaking through the new-growth woodlands.

Marcus drew his blanket around his shoulders. He slowly rose to his feet. He gave his scraggy beard a fierce scratch. He pulled a grimy, green woolen cap down tight over his ears. Long strands of greasy brown hair curled up around his shoulders.

He wore multiple layers of clothes: two T-shirts, a heavy flannel shirt, a bulky sweater, an overcoat, plus thermals under his sweat pants. Both of his big toes poked out of the same pair of holey socks he'd been wearing for the past two weeks straight.

He stepped into his boots with the cardboard inserts. He didn't have to bother tying them, as they didn't have shoelaces. He gathered up the tarp, his pillow made of packaging foam, and the threadbare blanket, and stuffed them in a battered shopping cart.

He then ducked behind a tree to urinate.

Ferreting in his overcoat pocket, he discovered a hard remnant of jerky. He slipped it into his mouth. He sucked on the tasty morsel, working up a savory juice. He swallowed, deceiving his stomach into thinking food would follow.

Marcus observed a man emerging from the front door of his home a short distance away on a block of luxurious houses. He wore dark sunglasses, a black jogging suit with white piping, and running shoes. He hustled down the walkway. He broke into a sprint and ran across the street into the park. He ran rhythmically, wearing earbuds and listening to music on the iPod cinched to his right bicep.

Marcus pulled back the frayed cuff of his tattered overcoat. He checked the time on a wristwatch he'd found in a trash bin. Despite the cracked crystal and kinked band, the timepiece was relatively accurate.

The jogger was right on schedule.

Marcus watched the man dash up a grassy knoll,

descend the other side, and dart past the perimeter of the construction site of an outdoor amphitheater. The jogger disappeared into the grove of cottonwoods separating the rural parkland from the neighboring string of houses.

Marcus pushed his shopping cart onto the sidewalk with no real destination in mind. What he hated most about being homeless was the wandering.

He knew how it felt to be scorned. Even the organizations that pledged to help the homeless had shunned him. On cold nights, he would stand in a line for hours, freezing to death, stomping his feet to stay warm outside of a shelter with hundreds of other poor souls, only to be told when he reached the doors that they were full.

Only on rare occasions would someone show a smidgen of compassion. They'd give him a thin blanket, a mat, and a space on the hard floor. The next morning, when six o'clock rolled around, he and the others would be ordered to vacate the premises and would be ushered back out onto the streets; shelters were places for sleeping, not for daytime congregations.

Stray mutts in animal shelters were given more respect. At least, during the day, they were provided with roofs over their heads and regular meals, if only for a short period. Marcus wondered how long it would take before the city began treating the homeless the same way they treated unwanted pets.

It seemed even the police despised him. If a couple were cuddling on a park bench, enjoying the day, and a cop strolled by, the officer would give them a pleasant smile and a kind greeting. But if Marcus rested on the same bench, and the same cop showed up, Marcus would be accused of vagrancy and told to move along.

He remembered the time he'd been so distressed, he'd actually walked into a police station and asked for help. One officer behind a counter had given Marcus a referral number and told him to use the payphone down the hall. Marcus might have considered making the call if he'd only had the money.

Soup kitchens meant standing in line for most of the day without any guarantee of receiving a meal. Often, he would reach the front of the line, only to be told they'd run out of food and that he should come back for the next scheduled mealtime. When he was fortunate to land a free meal, it was disconcerting how the stern-faced servers piled the scooped food onto his tray, like farm hands feeding slop to a hog.

If he didn't make a pest of himself, a few store owners would take pity on him. Sometimes his gray-toothed smile would earn him a sandwich or a beverage, and if his eyes became weepy, he might even score a small bag of groceries.

Panhandling was always degrading. If he wanted something hot to eat or drink, he needed money. Usually, he would pick a spot on a busy sidewalk or by a corner market. People who didn't have much to spare were usually gracious enough to hand over their change, maybe even a dollar. But the affluent? Those folks driving shiny SUVs? They were less generous.

When he wasn't begging, he'd scavenge the back alleys. Though he didn't make a habit of it, he'd resort to dumpster diving rather than starve to death—something he was not particularly proud of.

IN CASE OF CARNAGE

He could honestly attest to what it felt like to be a feral animal.

Like clockwork, he would wander the suburban streets before dusk, rummaging through garbage and recycling bins left out by the curb the night before collection day, the homeowners unaware of the unkempt stranger sifting through their discards. He would amass redeemable bottles and cans and exchange them for cash at recycling centers.

While Marcus scoured the garbage bins, he often came across carelessly discarded personal information—tax forms with social security numbers, bank statements with account numbers. It was shocking how people could be so incautious, jeopardizing their livelihoods, thinking no one would consider digging through their garbage to steal their identities. He often came across plastic bags full of shredded paper. He knew if someone were determined to spend the time, they could piece all that confetti back together again.

Marcus had few friends. Most days, Carl lay under his inverted "V" of cardboard, reading the previous day's newspaper. Carl had been a prominent college professor—or so he claimed.

Occasionally, Marcus bumped into Fast Eddie, so called because he spoke a million words a minute and never knew when to shut up. Marcus suspected Fast Eddie was a deranged, incurable heroin addict who was hooked on methadone.

There were others he recognized by face alone. Most homeless people kept their identities to themselves, as they didn't trust anyone, especially another tramp who might rob them of what little they had.

Every day, he thought of his wife, Kelly, and their daughter, Amy. He missed them. He wished they could be together.

At night, Marcus remained vigilant. Packs of mean-spirited teenagers roamed everywhere, getting their thrills by preying on the destitute.

Marcus had been beaten up once while he'd slept. A bottle had been smashed over his head. The heel of a heavy motorcycle boot had broken three of the fingers on his right hand. A length of pipe had fractured his nose and cracked two ribs.

The next morning, he'd walked into a free clinic and collapsed on the floor.

***

Late afternoon, Marcus returned to the suburban neighborhood by the park.

He was strolling along the sidewalk with his shopping cart when a garage door automatically rolled up. A shiny black BMW sedan backed out of the garage.

The jogger from that morning was behind the wheel. The driver checked the street both ways, then paused for a moment to stare at Marcus. He shook his head with disdain, whipping out of the driveway as the garage door closed. He sped off down the road.

An hour later, Marcus was sitting on a park bench with his right shoe and sock off, massaging his filthy foot, when the same BMW returned and drove into the garage.

Just before dusk, the jogger exited his house on his

normal jaunt. He sprinted across the street into the park.

It was almost nightfall, so there was no one in the park except for Marcus.

Marcus waited on the crest of the hill.

The jogger ran up the slope. "Hey! Get out of my way!" he snapped, darting around Marcus.

Marcus turned and held out his hand.

"Get a job, you miserable bum!" the jogger shouted, glaring over his shoulder.

The man collided with the shopping cart, sending it rolling. He clung to the front as it raced down the grassy hill toward the construction site. It sailed over the top of a cement retainer wall and plummeted twenty feet down on a concrete slab.

Three rebars speared through the jogger's chest as he landed on his back. The shopping cart crashed beside him.

Marcus climbed down and knelt beside the quivering man.

"Please . . . help me," choked out the jogger, wheezing his last breath. Blood oozed under his body.

Marcus foraged through the dead man's pockets. He found only a house key.

He righted the mangled shopping cart and gathered his strewn belongings. After reloading his cart, he parked it behind a bush.

Marcus left the body where the jogger had landed. A stack of cinder blocks hid it from anyone's view.

He trudged up the hill and glanced both ways before crossing the street, relieved there was no one around to see him. He scurried up the walkway to the jogger's front door, then let himself in with the dead man's house key.

Standing in the small foyer, Marcus took a moment. It was the first time in a very long while since he'd been inside a house. He glanced around the entry, admiring the marble floor, the crown molding, the recessed ceiling lighting, the warmth of the creamy beige walls.

On each side of the archway leading to the living room stood a tall fern in a ceramic pot.

Marcus stepped into the spacious room with its high-vaulted ceiling, reminding him of the inside of a cathedral. The owner was partial to black leather, as the couches, ottomans, and chairs were all fabricated from the same material. Oil paintings adorned the walls, mostly of frigates jostled by the high seas. Blue flames danced on the artificial logs in the gas fireplace.

A big-screen TV occupied much of one wall, which was bordered with bookcases stretching from the floor up to the ceiling.

Marcus entered the kitchen.

A woman stood at the counter with her back turned. She was barefoot, wearing an oversized T-shirt, the bottom skirting her tanned thighs. She'd obviously heard Marcus enter the house. "You're back early."

The woman turned. She looked at Marcus. She wasn't the least bit afraid. "Get your filthy ass out of my house! Get the hell out!" She grabbed a carving knife out of the block. In doing so, she accidentally swiped a wooden salad bowl off the counter. Lettuce, sliced tomatoes, and cucumbers spilled onto the floor.

Marcus put up his hands. "Put down the knife."

"Oh, yeah?" she sneered. "Get out!"

"Not until—"

IN CASE OF CARNAGE

The woman lunged. She swiped the blade across the front of his overcoat, narrowly missing Marcus as he stepped back. Still on the offensive, the woman thrust the stainless-steel point at Marcus's chest.

Marcus sidestepped her advance. He thrust his palm out at her shoulder, jolting her backwards. She slipped on the slick vegetables. Her right foot went out from under her. She struck the base of her skull on the edge of the granite countertop and slumped to the floor.

Marcus stood over her lifeless body. He watched a small crimson pool bloom around her head.

He continued his tour through the exorbitant house, climbing the stairs to the landing. He strolled down the hall, passing three doorways to separate bedrooms. He reached a double-door entry to an ornate, palace-sized master bedroom.

Marcus waltzed into the room. He strolled past the walk-in closet and directly into the bathroom. An enormous four-by-eight-foot mirror above a two-sink granite countertop covered one wall. A bay window accompanied the Jacuzzi, while the toilet graced its own space as if it were in a showroom. The shower stall could fit a horse.

Marcus stripped off his grungy clothes and tossed them into the bathtub.

He searched a vanity drawer for nail clippers and trimmed his finger and toenails. For twenty minutes, he leaned in front of the mirror, cutting his hair, then shaved off his beard.

In the shower, he turned the faucets full blast. He washed his hair, scrubbed the smirch from his body.

After toweling himself dry, he entered the bedroom

to search the dresser drawers. Naked, he paraded into the walk-in closet, admired the fine garments and shoes.

He found underwear and socks still in the packages. He picked out a pair of pleated slacks, a salmon polo shirt, and new loafers from a shoebox to wear.

On the bed, he meticulously arranged a week's worth of clothes he fancied. He packed them in a suitcase.

Marcus carried the suitcase downstairs, along with his old clothes, which were stuffed in a garbage bag. He placed them by the front door.

In the kitchen, he grabbed an apple out of the refrigerator. He looked at the dead woman lying in the bloody mess and took a bite from the apple.

Marcus munched on his apple as he discovered a home office. It looked more like a command center. Four computers occupied a long table with chairs, a large mahogany desk, a row of filing cabinets, and stacks of boxes.

He pulled open the top drawer in the desk. It was filled with credit cards, each with a different person's name on it.

Marcus sat down in a chair. He spent a few minutes delving through the plastic, then kept only two. He put the credit cards in an attaché case that was already on the table.

He opened the next drawer. He found checkbooks inside with the registers in individual leather cases. He kept two.

The third drawer was full of debit cards with their corresponding personal identification numbers. He stuffed one card into the briefcase, along with a battery-operated calculator.

IN CASE OF CARNAGE

In the bottom drawer, he found a shoebox. When he removed the lid, his face beamed; it was filled with fat stacks of hundred-dollar bills held together with rubber bands. He emptied the box into the attaché case.

Marcus went over to the file cabinets. He rifled through folders containing security bonds and stock certificates. He shut the drawer without taking any.

He checked a few more drawers, finding more valuables. He closed the full attaché case. He deposited it by the front door next to the suitcase and the garbage bag.

For dinner (while doing his best not to trip over the dead woman or step in her blood), Marcus broiled a thick rib eye steak. He fixed himself a couple of scotches from the wet bar, toasted the corpse on the floor, and with his supper, polished off what tasted like an expensive bottle of his host's merlot.

Instead of sleeping in the master bedroom, Marcus slept in one of the spare bedrooms. He set the alarm before drifting off. For the first time in the longest while, he was actually sleeping in a real bed with a full stomach and without the fear of freezing to death or being murdered in his sleep by some lunatic.

Come morning, Marcus was startled by the alarm clock, unaccustomed to the jarring sound. Golden sunlight filtered into the room. He rose out of bed and got dressed.

He devoted an hour to retracing his steps, making sure he wiped down everything inside the house he might have touched.

After opening the front door, Marcus rubbed his fingerprints off the knob with a handkerchief. He tucked the garbage bag under his arm, then picked up the suit-case and the attaché case. He stepped outside and pulled the door shut.

* * *

After tossing the garbage bag into a dumpster behind a 7-Eleven, Marcus caught a transit bus across town to a neighborhood of narrowly spaced two-story houses with step-up porches and run-down front yards.

He got off at the bus stop and headed down the street to a house on the corner. He strode up the steps to the front door and knocked.

A young woman opened the door. She took one look at Marcus and screamed, "Oh my God! Marcus!" She placed her hands on Marcus's cheeks. "Honey, we thought something happened to you! We've been so worried!"

"I know, Kelly. I'm sorry," Marcus apologized. He dropped the attaché case and the suitcase on the porch to embrace his wife.

"Where have you been?"

"On the streets."

"Doing what?"

"Searching for—"

"Daddy! Daddy!" an eight-year-old girl squealed, charging out of the house.

"Amy!" Marcus hugged his daughter, covering her head with kisses.

"Who's there? What's all the commotion?" an elderly woman hollered from inside the house.

"It's Marcus, Grandma! He's returned!" Kelly yelled,

tears rolling down her cheeks.

"Well, it's about time!"

Kelly gave her husband an incredulous look. "Marcus, do you realize you've been gone for nearly a year?"

"I know, but I couldn't give up. Not until I found them."

"Where did you get those clothes?"

"I'll explain later." Marcus handed the attaché case to Kelly.

"What's this?"

"Everything those creeps stole from us, down to the last penny. Finally, we have our identities back."

14
CASE NUMBER:
18-08-249

Hank checked his watch as they passed under the flickering neon light of the Speedy Mart & Gas. He noted the time at precisely eleven minutes after one in the morning. Bill parked the Crown Victoria in front of the convenience store.

"I'd kill for a coffee," Hank grumbled as he climbed out.

"Better make it a double homicide, and throw in some jelly donuts." Bill slammed his door.

They were immediately assaulted by a strange smell.

"Jeez! What is *that*?" Hank asked.

"Maybe a dumpster caught fire."

The detectives ambled over to Clare, who was hunkered by one of the gas pump islands where a flatbed truck, equipped with side panels and a lift gate, was parked.

"Hey, Clare," Hank greeted.

Clare peered over her shoulder, "CSI" lettered on the

back of her jacket. "Hey, guys."

"Jesus! What do we have here?" Hank caught his first glimpse of the molten shape baked on the bubbled tarmac.

Bill took a closer look. "He must have been a big man."

"Actually, it's *two* people," Clare corrected. "At least, I *think* it is."

"Oh, I see it now."

The charred bodies looked like two rubber action figures a kid had doused with lighter fluid and set on fire. It was impossible to determine where one body ended and the other began.

"Kind of looks like Rob Bottin's creature in *The Thing*," Bill said.

"It *does*, doesn't it?" Clare agreed.

"What are you guys talking about?" Hank looked at Clare for clarification.

"It's a horror movie. What, you never saw it?"

"I prefer Westerns."

Bill poked his thumb at his partner. "Hank doesn't like scary movies."

"They're just not my thing."

Bill and Clare exchanged glances, trying not to laugh at Hank's chance remark.

Hank stepped around the gas pump. The gas nozzle at the end of the hose lay near one of the blackened skulls.

A yellow evidence marker with the number "2" identified a charred Zippo lighter.

"Classic accident," Hank observed. "Fool lights up while the other guy's pumping gas, and they both go up in flames."

"Or it's a botched murder attempt," Bill quipped.

Clare shook her head. "I think I'll go with Hank's theory."

"You're always taking his side."

"That's because I'm the logical one." Hank gave Bill a smug look.

"Okay, Mr. Spock."

"Huh?"

"Jeez, Hank! Don't you watch *anything?*"

"You know, it's a miracle the entire gas station didn't go up," Hank said to Clare.

"A delay in the emergency shut-off closed the feed to the pump," Clare said. "Unfortunately, not in time to save these two."

Bill flipped open his notepad. "Have you determined time of death?"

Tendrils of smoke rose from the cremated mass.

"An hour ago," Clare said. "Maybe two." Milton has something he wants to show you guys inside the store."

"Can't be any freakier than this." Bill stepped back from the fused bodies.

"Oh, believe me. It is!"

Hank and Bill walked toward the front entrance of the convenience store. They passed a forensic investigator who was shining a flashlight on the pavement, searching for clues.

A uniformed patrolman sat in his cruiser, typing on his keyboard and detailing his report. Officer Silverman stood by the entrance door, which was cordoned off with yellow police tape. He lifted the tape so the detectives could duck beneath it. The automatic doors swished open.

IN CASE OF CARNAGE

The detectives entered the store, snapping on their gloves. Hank smelled a cloying odor he might expect if he stuck his head into a burlap sack filled with copper pennies, fermented fruit, and rancid meat. He made a quick visual sweep of the store.

In the first aisle, he saw a large puddle of brown liquid, broken glass, an empty shelf, and burst food boxes and dented cans swept onto the floor.

Milton stood on the other side of the checkout counter. He had a sprawling forehead and wore thick eyeglasses. He looked like a munchkin from *The Wizard of Oz*.

The smell seemed to be coming from Milton's direction. Bill wrinkled his nose. "Milton, did you fart?"

"Bill Hendrix, always the comedian. Remind me to laugh."

Hank stepped up to the counter. "So what do we have?"

"Well, we got this poor sap, for starters." Milton looked down at his feet.

Hank and Bill leaned over the counter.

The night clerk was on the floor.

"Where's his face?" Bill asked.

"Come around. I'll show you what happened."

The detectives eased behind the counter, careful not to step in the large pool of blood under the clerk's ravaged head.

Milton directed their attention to a monitor next to a tape recorder on a shelf below the register. "I've already rewound the surveillance tape after watching it," he said. "This is most bizarre."

The detectives watched the monitor while Milton started the tape. A black-and-white image of the store's interior appeared on the screen. The camera was positioned to capture the checkout stand and the front of the aisles.

A few seconds into the tape, a man lurched into the store. He staggered about, obviously disoriented. With his hands, he started batting things off the shelves and onto the floor like a big kid having a tantrum.

Bill half laughed. "The guy's obviously drunk! Too bad it doesn't have audio."

The clerk waved his arms and pointed at the intruder. It was clear he was ordering the man to leave. It was like watching an old-time silent movie when everyone comically overacted between subtitles.

The man turned with both arms extended in front of him. He marched stiffly toward the clerk.

Bill gawked at the screen. "What is this? A lost reel of *Night of the Living Dead?*"

"This has to be a joke." Hank was convinced it was all a prank—until the man grabbed both sides of the clerk's face and gnawed off his nose.

"No way!" Bill shouted.

It was like an overzealous pie-eating contestant— only it wasn't a raspberry pie his head was buried in; it was the clerk's bloody face.

When it became almost unbearable to watch, the cannibal attack ended.

The deranged man took a step back, cocked his head to the side as if something were crawling around inside his ear, and lumbered out of the store.

The monitor went black as the VCR automatically shut off.

Milton looked at the detectives. "Pretty creepy, wouldn't you agree?"

"I'll say," Hank said.

"That was definitely a zombie," Bill said.

"Get real, Bill. You just said he looked drunk."

"I changed my mind. We just witnessed a real, live zombie."

"First of all, there is no such thing." Hank kept shaking his head. "And second of all, isn't 'live zombie' an oxymoron?"

"I have to agree with Bill." Milton gave Hank a serious look. "We all saw it."

Hank eyed the two carafes on the twin hotplates—one labeled "Roasted," the other "Decaf"—desperate to swing the conversation in another direction. "Think the coffee's still good?"

Milton scowled at Hank. "I don't have to remind you this is still a crime scene."

"Have you dusted for prints?" Hank asked.

"Well, yes."

"Seems a shame when it's only going to get thrown out."

"I have to admit, it does sound tempting," Milton said. "Oh, what the hell."

Hank plucked three Styrofoam cups from a stack. He filled them with the roasted blend.

"You know, while we're at it . . ." Bill motioned to the display containing an assortment of bear claws, Danishes, and donuts.

"I'll have a chocolate glaze," Hank said.

Bill reached in and handed Hank the donut.

Milton pointed to a lemon Danish.

Bill bit his powdered sugar donut.

They sipped their coffees.

The entrance doors hissed open.

"What's going on in here?" Clare demanded, marching up to the counter.

The three men froze, each with a pastry in one hand and a coffee in the other.

Clare glared at them. She put her hands on her hips.

"Could we interest you in a Danish?" Hank feebly asked.

"And some decaf, if you have it," Clare replied, breaking into a grin.

***

Forty-five minutes later, Hank and Bill stood outside, each finishing his second cup of coffee, when a gray Chevy Suburban pulled into the station. A business plaque on the driver door read: Citywide Toxic Waste Management Disposal.

"That should be Mr. Clifton," Officer Silverman called over to the detectives.

A large man climbed out of the SUV. He strode over as if he wanted to clobber whoever had summoned him from bed at three in the morning. His scowl changed to mild surprise, then a tight-lipped smile when he saw the panel truck next to the gas pump island. "Great! You found my truck."

Hank handed the vehicle registration to Clifton. "Sorry to get you up at this time of night."

"So where is my lame-ass brother? Anthony and his jerk friend took off with this truck. I swear, when I get my hands on those two . . ." Clifton punched his fist into the palm of his hand.

"I'm afraid I have some bad news." Hank pointed to the charred bodies by the pumps. Clare was plucking a tissue sample for a DNA match.

"Oh, Jesus!" Clifton nearly keeled over. He leaned back against the truck and looked away.

Clare glanced up at the detectives. "This makes my job a lot easier."

Bill walked up to Clifton. "We believe your brother or his friend may have killed the convenience store clerk."

"My brother's a flake. He's no killer."

"Have you ever known him to go berserk?"

"No. Why?"

"Someone ate the clerk's face off. That's why."

"What? Like a frigging zombie?"

Bill glanced over at Hank. "*He* said it. *I* didn't."

"Let's be realistic here. We'll know which one did it after the lab work." Hank directed Clifton's attention back to the fused corpses. "It appears one of them decided to light up a cigarette while the other one was pumping, igniting the fumes."

Clifton turned away. He leaned against the truck, doubled over, and threw up on his shoes. He peered between the side paneling slats at the truck bed. "Oh, tell me they didn't."

"What's wrong?" Hank asked.

"It's gone!"

"What is?"

"The drum! The stupid bastards dumped the drum!"

***

After questioning Clifton, Hank and Bill returned to the station to catch up on some much-needed rest in the locker room lounge. Bill nodded off right away on the couch.

Every time Hank closed his eyes, he saw the gruesome image of the two burnt corpses. He decided to forego sleep to catch up on a backlog of work on his desk.

Bill staggered into the squad room just after noon. He plopped down in his chair.

"How'd you sleep?" Hank sat back, stretching his arms over his head.

"Like a stuffed pilgrim." Bill fished a chocolate-covered donut from the pink box on Hank's desk. "So, any luck with the truck log?"

"Yeah, I think we caught a break. The truck was serviced only a day ago. The mechanic recorded the odometer reading."

"Then we should be able to figure how many miles Clifton's brother put on the truck before arriving at the gas station." Bill licked the icing off the donut.

"Exactly. Based on the current reading, they traveled almost twenty-two miles."

"*That* should narrow it down."

Hank handed Bill a marked-up map.

"You drew in some lines here. Is this a road?" Bill asked.

"For a new tract of homes in development called Summit Estates up in the hills. I looked it up on the Internet. I would imagine it's pretty secluded."

"This would make for a perfect dumping site."

IN CASE OF CARNAGE

"And the mileage checks out."

* * *

The rural road wound up the canyon into the hills, which were clustered with giant mushroom-shaped oaks that towered over battlements of brushwood.

"Pretty good climb." Bill looked over at Hank as he slipped the Crown Victoria's transmission into low gear. "Still think they brought the truck all the way up here?"

"We'll see."

A massive granite sign that read "Summit Estates" stood on the side of the gravel road.

Bill pointed to a dirt road veering to the right. "Looks like tire tracks."

Hank gunned the powerful engine up the steep grade.

Once they reached the crest, Hank shut off the engine. They climbed out of the car.

Hank gazed out at the smog layer over the distant city below. "Can't say I really care for the view."

"Still, better to be up here than down there." Bill spotted an overturned barrel without the lid lying on its side in a yellowish green puddle. "Looks like your hunch paid off."

Hank got down on one knee to peer inside the drum. "What do you think it is? There wasn't a manifest in the truck's glove compartment when I checked last night."

"Damned if *I* know. Whatever it is, it must be toxic as hell."

Everything that came into contact with the sludge

181

was wilted or dead: grass, weeds, shrubs, two birds, and a toad.

"The lid must have burst off the drum when they pushed it off the truck," Hank said.

"Looks like one of them fell in." Bill drew Hank's attention to the hand imprint in the coagulated substance.

"I wonder if it was the one who killed the convenience store clerk."

"Be my guess." Bill took out his notepad. He wrote down the series of numbers that were stenciled on the drum under the skull-and-crossbones warning label and "Property of the U.S. Government."

"That's a fifty-five-gallon drum," Hank said. "Judging by the existing puddle, I'd say we're missing about fifty gallons."

The detectives walked a path parallel to a narrow trench stained with the mysterious chemical. They followed it to a ridge that overlooked the sprawling housing development site below.

A small cul-de-sac of five newly constructed homes was directly below, some with cars parked in the driveways. The other streets branching off were in early building stages, mostly concrete slabs and some framed shells.

The furrow of toxic goop trailed down the steep slope for about fifty feet, passing under a cyclone fence into a bean-shaped swimming pool.

The backyard was a mess of tipped over tables and chairs, uprooted plants, and shattered clay pots strewn about the patio. A chaise lounge and an air mattress were cast adrift in the pool.

Bill put his hand up to shield his eyes from the sun.

IN CASE OF CARNAGE

"Is that a body?"

"Looks like it."

A sunburned woman in a two-piece bathing suit floated face down in the middle of the pool.

***

Hank parked the Crown Victoria at the curb by the first of the houses that looped around the cul-de-sac. Cars were parked in the driveways, but there was no sign of the residents. With no shade trees to block the afternoon sun, every house was a mirage shimmering behind the heat wave rising off the sidewalk.

Getting out of the car, Bill shrugged out of his suit jacket. He tossed it over the headrest. He unbuttoned his shirtsleeves and rolled them up just below the elbows, then loosened his tie.

Hank exited his side. "Captain sees you looking like that, he'll bust you back to a beat cop."

"You want to sweat to death, be my guest."

"What the hell." Hank took off his jacket.

"Is it me, or is this place a ghost town?" Bill asked.

A woman screamed from inside a house directly across the street from the one with the pool.

The detectives cut across a newly planted lawn. They ran up the steps to the front entrance. Hank pounded on the door. "Police! Open up!"

Again, a scream, only this time it was cut short.

Bill raised his right leg. He kicked the doorknob. Hank followed through with his shoulder, busting open the door.

A loud crash rumbled from the second floor.

Hank and Bill charged up the staircase, drawing their weapons.

After reaching the landing, Hank sidled up to the left wall of the hall, while Bill kept to the right side.

Strange noises gurgled from the room at the end of the hall, like someone blowing bubbles in a bucket of water. The detectives crept up to the master bedroom.

A naked elderly woman was face up on a king-size bed. Her intestines dangled out of her exposed belly and coiled onto a lamp, which was shattered on a small throw rug.

A scrawny old man in black swim trunks was leaning over the woman, his head buried inside her stomach. Their red, blistered bodies looked as if they had been scalded by a hot shower.

Hank swallowed hard, fighting back the urge to puke.

"If this is what geriatric foreplay looks like," Bill said, "you can count me out."

"Not funny, Bill."

The old man arched his back, raising his gore-covered head out of the woman's desecrated stomach. He turned to the detectives, his rheumy eyes peering out from behind a crimson mask. He puffed out a rush of air, vibrating his lips like a horse. Tiny pink bubbles dappled his chin. He shook his head, flicking bloody mist everywhere.

The old man leaped off the bed. He moved with an incredible speed that was unnatural for a person his age. He vaulted across the room.

With no time to issue a warning, Hank fired two times. Both shots penetrated the man's chest without any effect.

IN CASE OF CARNAGE

Bill shot the man point-blank in the face.

The man stumbled blindly out of the bedroom and into the hall. He slammed into the railing and soared over the banister. His skull sounded like an exploding melon from the fifteen-foot fall.

They stepped into the master bedroom to take a closer look at the woman.

She couldn't have been more ravaged if she'd been attacked by a fierce pack of hungry wolves.

Hank turned away, having seen enough. "Why would anyone do such a thing?"

"I'll call it in." Bill reached into his trouser pocket. "Damn! I left my cell phone in my jacket. You bring yours?"

"It's in my coat."

"Christ. Let's get back to the car."

The detectives scampered downstairs and hurried out the front door.

The trunk of the Crown Victoria was open.

Bill looked at Hank. "Seriously? Someone broke into our car?"

Hank and Bill advanced slowly toward the vehicle.

Two men in bathing suits stepped out from behind the car. Their skin looked baked to a crisp, as if they had fallen asleep inside tanning booths.

One man ratcheted a police-issue Remington 12-gauge pump he'd stolen from the cruiser's trunk.

"Put it down before we put *you* down!" Bill shouted.

The man with the shotgun grinned. He turned to the man standing next to him. He rested the muzzle of the shotgun on the bridge of the other man's nose and pulled the trigger.

The victim's head exploded in a scarlet mist.

"That is seriously messed up!" Bill yelled. "Since when do zombies use guns?"

The man with the shotgun cocked another shell into the chamber.

The detectives dove behind a hedge.

The shotgun blast shredded the leaves off the top of the bush, sending mulch raining down on their heads.

Hank and Bill scurried through an open gate next door. They ran down the side yard. The rear sliding glass door was unlocked, so they slipped into the house.

The kitchen was snow-blind white: white cabinets, white counter tiles, white appliances.

The red pool of blood on the white linoleum floor screamed to be noticed.

Bill peeked out through the sliding glass door. "I don't see him coming."

Bare footprints tracked through the blood and led out of the kitchen.

The detectives didn't have to look far to see a dead man halfway down the hall.

He was flat on his back, sporting a pair of Hawaiian swim trunks, a meat cleaver wedged in his forehead. His skin looked overcooked, as if he'd been roasted on a rotisserie spit.

They heard a scuffling noise coming from behind a door in the kitchen.

Bill pointed his gun at the door. "Someone's in the pantry."

Hank grabbed the doorknob. He opened the door about six inches.

IN CASE OF CARNAGE

A carving knife thrust out in a stabbing motion. Hank kicked the door, slamming it into the attacker's wrist. The blade clattered to the floor. A voice cried out inside the pantry.

Hank swung open the door.

A young woman cowered in the back of the pantry. She wore a yellow T-shirt, a pair of jeans, and white sneakers. As she was a redhead, her face was freckled and porcelain white.

"Well, I guess it's safe to assume you're not one of them." Hank lowered his gun. "What's your name?"

"Sherry. Sherry Thompson."

"You live here?"

"Yes. It's just me and my husband."

"Is that him in the hall?"

Sherry stepped out of the pantry and glanced down the hall. "Oh my God!" Sherry broke into tears. "He gave me no choice. He came at me like a madman!"

Bill showed her to a chair. "Maybe you should tell us what happened."

"The Andersons invited everyone on the block over for a pool party. I wasn't feeling up to it. Earl insisted we go." Sherry paused for a moment, the reality of what she had done finally hitting her.

"That's okay. Take it slow," Hank said reassuringly.

"I had a splitting headache. Earl could be such a pest when he wanted his way, so I just gave in. We were probably the last ones to come over. Just about everyone was already in the pool. Charles—Mr. Anderson—was complaining that his pool filter wasn't working properly. There was this yellowish cloud in the water at the deep end. Looked like pee. It was pretty gross."

"So I gather you didn't go swimming?" Hank asked.

"No. I only stayed about fifteen minutes. Then I came home to lie down."

"Lucky for you," Bill said.

"I got up to get a glass of water. The next thing I knew, Earl was behind me with his hands around my throat. I thought he was going to kill me. I remember grabbing the meat cleaver . . ." She paused and took a deep breath. "Why would he want to hurt me?"

Hank glanced over at Bill. "Are you thinking what I'm thinking?"

"Must be a reaction to that chemical in the pool," Bill said.

Sherry gave the detectives a questioning look.

"Some idiots dumped a drum full of a liquid chemical up on the hill," Bill said. "The spill drained down into the Andersons' pool."

"And that's what made Earl go crazy?" Sherry asked.

"We think so," Hank said. "How many people were at this pool party, would you say?"

"Counting myself, twelve."

"And everyone went in the pool?" Hank took his notepad out of his shirt pocket to make a list.

"All except me."

"Eleven, huh? We were forced to shoot the man next door, who we believe killed his wife," Hank said.

"You mean Mitch and Lois?"

"I'm afraid so." Hank wrote down their names.

"They were the sweetest couple."

Bill shook his head. "Not anymore. We saw a dead

woman floating in the pool."

"What was she wearing?"

"A green two-piece bikini."

"Oh my God! Maggie!"

"Who is Maggie?" Hank asked.

"Maggie and Donald live two houses over. They have a six-year-old daughter, Cindy."

"I was hoping there wouldn't be any kids," Bill said.

"The Andersons have a teenage boy, Joey."

"Who else was there?" Hank asked.

"Rob and Carl."

Hank jotted the names. "Tall guys, buff builds?"

"Yeah, they're carpenters."

"Do they have guns?" Bill asked.

"I know they hunt."

"We can scratch one of them off the list." Hank put question marks behind each name. "Anyone else?"

"There's Charles Anderson and his wife, Catherine. Oh, wait. Does the Andersons' dog count?"

"Was it in the water?" Hank asked.

"Joey kept throwing Hercules's toys in the pool to fetch. Charles got all over him."

"What breed of dog?"

"Hercules is a huge rottweiler."

Bill let out an exasperated breath.

"What's wrong?"

"Let's just say Hank and I aren't fond of big dogs." Bill glanced over at Hank. "So what's the tally?"

Hank consulted his notes. "I'm counting five dead, which leaves six people who are possibly infected, eliminating Sherry."

Hank walked across the small kitchen. He grabbed the phone off the wall and pressed the receiver to his ear. "The phone's dead."

"Do you have a cell phone?" Bill asked Sherry.

"Earl took mine to the party, as his needed to be charged."

"There's no other phone in the house?" Hank asked.

"No, I'm sorry. There isn't."

"That only leaves our car radio." Hank glanced down the hall.

Earl was sitting up. His skin was red as molten lava. He grabbed the handle of the meat cleaver. He rocked the blade back and forth and yanked it from his forehead.

"We have a serious problem," Hank said.

Bill and Sherry witnessed the man they had presumed dead rise to his feet.

"Oh my God, Earl! You're alive!" Sherry's voice was a mixture of relief and dread.

Bill watched bewildered. "Your husband must have a thick skull."

Sherry's husband's face was beet red, the whites of his eyes fluorescent.

"Honey, everything is going to be okay. These are policemen."

"Put the meat cleaver down! *Now!*" Bill ordered.

"You heard him!" Hank shouted.

Instead of heeding their warnings, Earl advanced toward the kitchen. It was strange watching him walk as though he were a toddler, unsure of himself, taking his first steps. His face drooped as if he might cry. He worked his jaw, as if chewing on the words, and uttered, "You know, Sherry, you really hurt me."

"I'm sorry, baby."

"Yeah, you'll be sorry!" Earl charged into the kitchen and ran straight for Sherry, raising the meat cleaver over his head, ready to strike.

Bill knocked Earl up against the wall.

The meat cleaver swung down, narrowly missing Bill as he stepped out of the way.

Earl kept swinging the blade.

Hank shot him point-blank in the chest.

Sherry screamed.

Earl stumbled back. He gave his head a quick shake, as if he were clearing his mind. He raised the meat cleaver.

Bill pressed the muzzle of his .38 against Earl's temple and pulled the trigger.

Earl careened off the kitchen table and onto the floor.

"Let's get out of here." Hank led the way out of the kitchen. He turned into the living room. Instead of going directly to the front door, he decided to peek between the curtains to see if the shotgun-toting maniac was still out there, waiting to ambush. "Oh, this isn't good."

Bill and Sherry came over to peer out the window. A fiery ball of black smoke engulfed the Crown Victoria.

***

"You're not safe here alone. You'd better come with us," Hank told Sherry.

Bill kept a vigilant watch through the window. "I don't see anyone."

"All right. Let's go see if the phone's working next door." Hank exited through the backway and started up the side of the house.

"Hank, wait!" Bill stopped him. "He might be waiting for us out front. Let's take a shortcut." Like a mule, Bill did a side kick, knocking out a fence board. He ripped two more boards out.

They squeezed through the opening and into the adjacent backyard.

The sliding glass door was wide open. Hank made sure the coast was clear, then stepped inside. "It's okay."

Bill strode directly to the kitchen phone. He picked up the receiver, shook his head. "They must have cut the main feed."

Suddenly, they heard running footsteps outside.

"Whose house is this again?" Hank whispered to Sherry.

"Rob and Carl's, the carpenters I told you about."

"Go, go!" Hank shouted, backing out of the kitchen.

Bill and Sherry dashed down a hallway.

"Hey, assholes!" the man yelled, stomping into the kitchen. He pumped a round into the shotgun he had taken from the Crown Vic. He was the spitting image of Ron Perlman's character, Hellboy, with the lobster-red skin but without the devilish sawed-off horns.

Bill opened a door leading into the garage. "Where's the opener?"

"To your right." Sherry pointed to a spot next to the furnace.

Hank shut the door.

Bill pressed the button on the wall.

They rushed toward the garage door.

The roll-up door didn't move.

"Damn! They must have cut the electricity." Hank looked around for somewhere to hide.

A Chevy Sierra was parked on one side of the two-car garage. On the other side was a workbench with enough tools to stock a small hardware store. A workout area was set up with a weight-training bench, a treadmill, and a rack of dumbbells next to a full-length mirror on the wall. A large steel utility box was on the cement floor—the type normally mounted behind the cab in the bed of a pickup truck.

The door leading into the garage exploded in a loud flurry of woodchips.

"Hey! Dickheads!" the infected man growled. He stepped into the garage, pushing aside the door with the gaping hole. Fresh cartridges were stuffed inside the waistband of his swim trunks. He drew back the slide, pumping another shell into the chamber. There was a shuffling sound behind the truck. He turned toward it and fired, blowing out the passenger window.

Bill appeared on the other side of the garage, holding his gun down by his side. "From where I'm standing, I'd say *you're* the dickhead."

The crazed man shot Bill.

Bill shattered into a thousand shiny shards.

Then the real Bill stepped out from behind the truck, no longer casting his image on the full-length mirror.

Hank popped up from behind the utility box.

The detectives dropped the man before he could fire another shot.

Sherry pushed open the truck door with her foot.

She was covered with chips of safety glass.

Hank holstered his gun and helped Sherry out of the truck. "You okay?"

"I thought he had us for sure."

Bill checked the man's pulse to make sure he was dead. "Well, now we only have five to worry about."

***

As there was no longer the threat of being gunned down in the street, they went back into the house and out the front door.

Hank glanced over at Sherry. "Donald and his daughter live next door?"

"That's right," she said.

Bill put away his gun. "What if the little girl is infected? I wouldn't have the heart to shoot her."

"We can lock her in a room or something," Hank said.

"Donald's a really nice guy," Sherry said. "Such a devoted father. I'd hate to see him get hurt."

"You saw what happened to your husband," Bill said. "For all we know, this chemical could be a contagion. One bite and . . ."

"Jesus, Bill. These aren't zombies," Hank said.

"Don't be so sure."

When they came to the next house, the front door wasn't closed all the way.

Hank took a quick peek inside. "Sherry, call into the house."

"Donald? Cindy? It's Sherry! You guys want to come out?"

IN CASE OF CARNAGE

There was no answer from inside the house.

"They must still be over at the Andersons'," Sherry said.

Bill glanced through a window. "Think we should check anyway?"

"I like our odds better out here." Hank closed the door.

They took a shortcut across the lawn and let themselves into the Andersons' house.

Whole mushrooms, chopped meat cubes, and green bell pepper slices trailed across the floor into the kitchen, ending at a chubby kid's head, where the pointy end of a stainless-steel skewer protruded from his ear canal.

The pudgy boy wore a pair of wet swim trunks and only one flip-flop. His entire body was a crimson rash from the chemical burn.

Sherry gasped. "Oh my God! It's Joey!"

Bill removed the tablecloth from the kitchen table and covered the boy.

Hank drew his revolver. "This might be a good time to reload."

Bill had brought along the 12-gauge. He fished some cartridges out of his trouser pocket and inserted them into the feed.

Hank ejected the spent shells from his .38 and inserted six new rounds with the speedloader.

Sherry sniffed. "Do you smell that?"

Bill took a whiff. "Smells like someone's barbecuing."

They walked out onto the backyard patio.

The back lawn was littered with party supplies, canned drinks, and tossed-about furniture. A shed stood beneath a cluster of shade trees. A very large doghouse nestled along the fence.

Maggie floated in the middle of the pool.

A burly, shirtless man in a pair of baggy shorts stood in front of a stainless-steel barbecue with his back turned. His skin was Martian red.

A couple of ice chests, both lids propped open, were by his feet.

"Charles?" Sherry called out.

Charles didn't respond.

They moved a little closer. Sherry took another step toward her neighbor. "Charles? Where's Catherine?"

Not bothering to turn around, Charles grumbled, "She's cooking."

"We didn't see her in the kitchen," Sherry said.

Charles raised a metal tool. He clanged it across the grill.

"Sir?" Bill said. "Where is your wife?" He kept his gun trained on the man.

"Cooking, I told you!" Charles turned. He gripped the handle of a machete.

A large shank of meat cooked on the grill.

Hank glanced down at the contents of one of the ice chests. "Christ almighty! He's chopped up his wife!"

"Hi, Sherry."

Sherry turned toward the voice. A little girl in a bathing suit stood near the shed. She looked like a fairy powdered with red pixie dust.

"Cindy? Are you okay?" Sherry stepped toward the girl.

"Sherry, be careful," Bill warned.

A man stepped out from behind the shed. His skin was flaming red. His wild hair made him look like a madman.

Sherry was caught by surprise. "Donald, it's okay. We want to help you."

Donald snatched up his daughter. He dangled her off the ground by her hair as if she were a Barbie doll.

"Donald, stop!" Sherry cried. "Put her down!"

Bill aimed the shotgun. He took a bead on the father. "You heard the lady. Put the kid down!"

Donald snarled, tossing his daughter to the ground. He dashed back behind the shed.

"Cindy, are you hurt?" Sherry rushed over to the little girl.

Cindy sat up, one hand behind her back.

"It's okay. No one is going to hurt you." Sherry knelt beside Cindy. "See? We just want to help—"

Cindy swung her tiny arm around, driving a meat skewer into Sherry's stomach. She yanked out the thin steel.

Grabbing her belly, Sherry slumped onto her side and curled up into a ball.

The little girl stepped away, laughing.

Bill rushed over to help Sherry.

Donald appeared from behind the shed. He swung a heavy mallet, striking Bill across the shoulder and causing him to drop the shotgun.

Bill immediately went down, landing on his back. He drew his .38.

Donald smashed Bill's hand with the mallet, knocking the revolver away. The gun clattered across the cement patio into the pool.

Donald raised the mallet once more.

A huge shape charged from behind a tree and

attacked Donald. The enormous rottweiler ripped into the man with its powerful teeth. The dog's eyes were as red as cherry tomatoes. Yellow drool foamed at its mouth—a good indicator that the canine was infected.

The massive dog turned on the detectives.

Donald crawled away toward the shed, taking advantage of the distraction.

Bill clutched his bruised shoulder with his sprained hand. He scooted backward across the patio.

Hank was preparing to shoot the dog when Charles lunged at him with an ice chest.

Turning his gun on Charles, Hank fired, trying his best for a headshot. When the ice chest blocked his target, he shot Charles in the groin, figuring that would stop him for sure.

Charles kept coming, ignoring the devastating injury, the front of his swim trunks blotched red. Blood streamed down his hairy legs and onto his bare feet.

After firing his last round, Hank dropped his .38. He reached down for his backup piece.

Charles threw the cooler.

It sailed over Hank and landed in the pool with a big splash. Hank drew his .380 as Charles came at him wielding the machete. Stepping back, Hank realized he was at the edge of the pool. His only option was to get on the diving board.

The platform bounced as he climbed up. Each backward step caused the board to bounce more.

Charles swung the machete.

Hank's heels jutted over the edge of the board. He fired his gun.

Charles's head stuttered back with each shot. The big man belly flopped onto the diving board, leaving Hank only standing room.

Suddenly, he was bouncing up and down. Hank bent his knees, keeping pace with the wobbling platform, not wanting to lose his balance and fall into the toxic water. He couldn't have been more afraid if he were teetering on the edge of the Grand Canyon.

Once the diving board was steady, Hank called over to Bill. "How're you doing?"

"Not so dandy, buddy." Bill staggered toward the edge of the pool.

Cindy came up behind Bill and stabbed him in the back of the thigh with the meat skewer.

He twisted around.

She yanked out the cooking tool and stabbed him in the other leg.

"Jesus, kid! What the hell!" Bill stumbled back. He slipped on the wet cement, went down, rolled over the edge into the pool—and landed on the air mattress.

He held on frantically, trying not to flip over. His shoes were soaking wet. When he lifted his feet, he heard his .380 automatic fall into the water. He stared down into the chlorinated water, watching his gun sink to the bottom of the pool.

Cindy got down on her knees. She jabbed the sharp tip of the meat skewer at the air mattress, hoping to pop it. Bill jerked away, causing the air mattress to drift beyond her reach.

"Hold on. I'll help you." Hank raised one foot to cross over Charles's prone body.

Hercules clambered onto the diving board with his massive front paws.

"Get off, you damn dog!" Hank yelled.

The brute dog jolted to a stop. A long, heavy-duty chain was attached to its collar; the other end of the chain was wrapped around a tree trunk. Hercules strained forward, slipping the chain one inch closer to the detective.

Hank knelt on Charles's shoulder blades, eye-to-eye with the beast.

Cindy knew enough to stay clear of the infected animal. She tiptoed around the edge of the pool. The demented girl taunted Bill, squatting to stir the lethal tip of the meat skewer in the water.

"What now?" Bill asked, floating helplessly out in the middle of the pool.

Hercules snarled. The dog tugged on the chain, edging another inch closer to Hank, who was teetering on the edge of the diving board.

"I guess we wait and see what happens."

***

Lately, Clare's cases had been a living nightmare. Well, not exactly *living*, as all of her work generally revolved around the deceased. It exhausted her just to look at the workload piled on her desk. The past few weeks, the durations of her shifts ranged anywhere from ten to twelve hours.

This place is turning me into a walking zombie.

It was a wonder she remembered where she lived; she spent so much time at the station. At least she hadn't forgotten Bill's special day, which was—

Oh my God! It's tonight!

She rushed over to her personal locker and grabbed the gift bag inside, then checked her watch. There was a slight chance Bill might still be a work. She wanted desperately to give him his present before he left.

Clare bolted out of her office and dashed down the hall.

When she reached the squad room, only a couple detectives were sitting at their desks, neither of them Bill.

"Damn," she grumbled, walking over to Bill's desk.

"What's up?"

Clare turned and spotted Todd Silverman strolling into the office. He was off duty, wearing his civvies: a short-sleeved cotton shirt hanging out of his blue jeans and a pair of sneakers. She could see the telltale bulge of his service revolver under his shirt at the beltline.

"I was hoping . . . You haven't seen Bill and Hank around, have you?"

"Nope. Why?"

"I wanted to—"

The phone rang on Hank's desk.

"Think we should get it?" Clare asked Todd.

"Sure. Why not? Take a message."

Clare picked up the phone. "Hello? Oh, hi, Jackie. No, Hank's not here at the moment." Clare paused to listen for a few seconds. "If I see him, I'll tell him you called. Okay. Bye." Clare scrunched her brow.

"What's wrong?"

"That was Hank's wife. She was expecting Hank to be home a couple of hours ago. She tried his cell phone, even called Bill's. No one's returned her calls. She sounded worried."

"Maybe Hank left a note on his desk." Todd leafed through a few papers, careful not to disturb anything. "No, I don't see anything."

"He left his computer on." Clare hit a button on the keyboard. An image appeared on the screen of a new housing project in development. "What's this?"

Todd leaned in to look at the screen. "That's Summit Estates. My sister Sherry and her husband bought a place up there."

"You want to go check it out?"

"Sure, I'll drive."

* * *

Todd gunned his candy-apple-red Mustang Shelby up the steep hill and turned into the building site. "Did I tell you I was studying for the detective's exam?"

"No. That's great!" Clare patted the young recruit on the shoulder.

On each block, the houses were in a different stage of development: on some blocks, the houses were already roofed, while on other blocks, the houses were only wood frames.

Todd and Clare followed a street to a group of homes that were already occupied. As soon as they arrived at the cul-de-sac, they knew something was wrong.

"Is that Bill and Hank's car?" Todd pointed to the smoldering wreckage on the U-shaped tarmac.

Clare bolted from the car, drawing her Glock. Todd

climbed out of his side, reaching under his shirt for his service revolver.

"Holy cow, Clare! Take look at that!" Todd pointed at the headless corpse in the swim trunks lying on the pavement.

Clare looked over at the last house. "Let's see if there's anyone inside."

They followed a walkway up to the front door. The door was half open. Clare stuck her head in and called out, "Police! Is there anyone inside the house?"

No one answered.

They entered the home. Todd and Clare crossed the living room, then stopped when they saw something covered with a tablecloth on the kitchen floor.

Todd lifted the cover. He gasped when he saw the bright red, chubby-faced boy with the steel skewer rammed into his ear canal.

A dog growled outside.

Clare and Todd stepped onto the backyard patio. They were shocked to see Bill floating on an air mattress next to a dead woman who was floating face down in the middle of the pool. A rottweiler was straining at its chain, clambering over a large man who was slumped on a diving board. It was trying to get to Hank, who was trapped on the other end. There was another woman lying on the grass, the lower portion of her shirt covered with blood.

"Oh my God!" Todd cried out. "That's Sherry!" He immediately ran across the lawn.

Clare walked toward the dog.

The rottweiler glared at her. Its eyes were so red, they seemed to be on fire.

"Careful, Clare!" Hank warned. "The dog's mad."

"Here, boy. Nice doggie." Clare waved her hand.

The rottweiler bounded off the diving board. Clare ran toward the tree. She cut to her left like a football receiver evading a tackle. The big dog lumbered after her. She kept circling the tree, duping the animal. Soon the chain wrapped completely around the tree. Clare kept the tree trunk between herself and the savage beast. She took out her tactical knife and wedged the blade between two links, preventing the chain from unraveling, should the dog decide to backtrack.

The rottweiler fought the chain. It clamped its jaws around the chain to free itself. After breaking a tooth, it quickly resigned itself to its fate and rested in the grass.

Hank staggered off the diving board. He picked up the long pole of a swimming pool leaf skimmer. "Bill! Grab hold!" He extended the pole across the water. Bill grabbed the end. Hank pulled him over to the edge.

"How'd you find us?" Bill asked Clare once he was on the cement.

"Just a little simple detective work," Clare said over her shoulder as she ran over to assist Todd, who was on his cell phone calling for an ambulance.

Sherry smiled up at her brother.

"Don't worry. Help's on the way," Todd said.

Cindy came out from behind the shed. She ran up to Todd, wielding the steel skewer and aiming for the back of his neck.

"No you don't, you little pixie!" Hank snared the little girl's head with the net on the end of the pole. He led her over to the shed, opened the door, and shoved her inside.

He closed the door, making sure the lock was on the clasp.

Cindy screamed, pounding on the aluminum walls.

"I bet you're glad *that's* over," Clare said to the detectives.

"Not quite," Bill replied.

"There's another one. The little girl's father." Hank dropped the pole. He stooped to pick the shotgun off the grass. "Okay, Donald, you can come out."

"We know you're back there." Bill hobbled around the side of the shed to flush the man out. "Hank, I don't see him."

Donald jumped down from the tree like a primal ape. He threw the mallet at Hank. The tool just missed Hank's head.

Hercules grabbed Donald's leg in its mouth. It chomped down, snapping the bone. Donald screamed as he was being mauled.

Hank shot the crazed dog.

Everyone turned to the welcoming sound of approaching sirens.

CASE NUMBER: 18-08-250

The Crossroads was jam-packed, every table and booth taken, leaving the other patrons only standing room. Hank weaved through the crowded bar, trying his best not to spill a drop of beer from the brim-full pitcher.

A guy with a beard bumped into Hank, jabbing him in the ribs with an elbow. Foam sloshed over the rim. Ice-cold suds drizzled on his hand, seeping under the cuff of his dress shirt.

Hank looked over, expecting an apology.

Not bothering to look back, the guy disappeared into the crowd.

Hank managed to maneuver to the booth away from the main bar near the pool tables without spilling another drop. He placed the pitcher on the table where Jackie,

Clare, and Bill sat. He slid in next to Jackie.

Bill hoisted the pitcher and topped off everyone's beer glasses.

The back door was propped open, as the air conditioner was on the fritz. They didn't have to shout to be heard and could carry on a decent conversation, as it was less noisy in the back, except for the clacking of the billiard balls.

Hank grabbed a few pretzels from the bowl on the table. "Anyone hear how Todd's sister is doing?"

"Todd called me. Says she's doing fine," Clare said. "Did I tell you Todd's going for the detective's exam?"

"Good for him." Bill took a gulp of his beer.

Hank looked over at Bill. "So, how're *you* doing?"

Bill held up his bandaged hand. "Three broken fingers, and the shoulder still hurts." He squirmed on the bench seat. "It's a little uncomfortable to sit, thanks to the kid playing Pin the Tail on the Donkey. The next pool party, let's not forget the sunscreen," Bill said, referring to their sunburned faces.

Hank took a sip of his beer. He glanced about the barroom and recognized the same jerk who'd bumped into him.

The man hunkered down with two other rough-looking characters in a booth next to the men's room door.

Hank tapped Bill's arm and nodded toward the three men. "You recognize them?"

Bill studied them for a moment. "Probably undercover from uptown."

Clare gulped down the last dregs in her glass. She grabbed the pitcher, filled her glass back up. "Did you hear the Feds indicted another CEO of an investment firm for embezzling?"

"Good for them," Bill said. "Greedy bastards. They screw people over and still walk away with those ridiculous golden parachutes."

"They're so big now, they're calling them *platinum* parachutes," Clare said.

"They should appoint *me* as the CEO parachute rigger. Let *me* pack those chutes. I'd like to see the looks on their faces when they pulled the rip cord." Bill laughed, raising his glass for everyone to take a drink.

"Aren't *you* the harsh one?" Clare licked the froth off her upper lip.

"Think *that's* harsh? I read, somewhere in some country, they lined up the managers of a company that was doing poorly and executed them in the parking lot."

Jackie rolled her eyes at Bill. "You're making that up."

"No, I swear. You know what really frosts my butt?"

"Winter?" Hank grinned. He poured the rest of the beer from the pitcher into everyone's glass.

"Very funny. No, all those poor folks who lost their 401ks. I mean, who can figure it out? The Fed comes in, bails out the banks, and what happens? The chairmen of the boards give the money to their executives as bonuses, when *they're* the ones who screwed up the economy in the first place. And, if that's not bad enough, they say the banks need a nice little cushion, just in case they mismanage everyone's money again."

"Maybe you should go into politics," Clare said.

"You think?" Bill glanced at the empty pitcher. "I'd

get the next one, but . . ." Bill held up his injured hand.

"Hold on a sec." Hank looked over at the three men.

The one with the beard was getting up to use the men's room. He was carrying a gym bag.

The other two men ducked their heads under the table.

Hank peered out the opened back doorway. The night sky was sprinkled with stars glinting around a full moon.

A loud howl sounded from within the men's room. The door sprang open, and out stepped a werewolf carrying a short-barreled Ithaca combat shotgun. The creature fired a quick burst into the ceiling to get everyone's attention.

Two werewolves jumped up from under the table, each with Desert Eagle .357 magnum pistols. They swept their gun muzzles about the bar, eager to shoot anyone who stood in their way.

Everyone in the bar stopped talking, as though a bustling beehive had suddenly been silenced, and turned to the rear of the bar.

A pool cue clattered onto the floor.

* * *

Hank and Bill stood over the three bodies lying on the barroom floor in a lake of blood. Each corpse was riddled with bullets, as if they'd been mown down with a fifty-caliber machine gun. The smoky bar reeked of battle.

Clare stood protectively next to Jackie, who was still seated at the booth.

"Talk about stupid," Bill said.

"I'll say," Hank agreed.

"Dumb bastards, is what they were," someone sounded off.

The detectives turned to face the forty-some other people, each of them pointing a handgun. Hank and Bill holstered their .38 snub-nosed revolvers.

Bill adjusted his party hat. "For a second there, I thought you guys were pulling a prank."

"Just another surprise for the birthday boy," Hank said.

"I mean, really, what were they thinking?" Bill reached down and removed a werewolf mask from one of the dead men. "Trying to rob a cop bar."

16
CASE NUMBER: 18-09-251

Hank and Bill stepped out of the captain's office with drooping heads. They went back to their desks and slumped in their chairs.

"He reamed us good," Hank said with an exasperated sigh.

"I'll say," Bill replied. "He ripped us a new one."

"He's just scared."

"That's the fifth Heavenly Donuts. Who torches donut shops, anyway?"

"A whacko, that's who!"

"That leaves only one store."

The captain stomped out of his office, clutching a powdered jelly donut. A strawberry blob clung to the belly of his rumpled shirt. "Hendrix! Jenkins!"

The detectives popped out of their chairs.

"I just got off the phone with the mayor. Says we don't catch this arsonist, he's calling the governor to send in the National Guard."

The captain marched back into his office.

Bill looked at Hank. "Is he serious? The National Guard?"

"I hear the mayor's big on morning staff meetings. The guy loves his Heavenly Donuts."

"Must be why he blocked all those other franchises. When's the last time you saw a Dunkin' Donuts, a Krispy Kreme, or a Starbucks? Not in *this* town."

"All the more reason to make sure nothing happens to the last Heavenly Donuts store. Can you imagine this town without donuts?"

Bill shuddered at the thought. "What would be the point of a cup of coffee if you couldn't have a donut?"

"Man can't start his day, he doesn't have his donut!"

"This is war!"

"Damn straight!"

Hank got on the horn with the dispatcher to send every available squad car over to the Heavenly Donuts store, while Bill phoned the SWAT commander.

Everyone in the office, including the captain, charged out of the squad room, armed to the teeth.

***

Thirty minutes later, the last standing Heavenly Donuts store looked like a bunker under siege.

The entire building was fortified with sandbags and armed military-clad SWAT officers.

Sharpshooters assembled on the roof.

An armored vehicle blocked one end of the street,

while a fire truck and a firemen brigade stood by, in case of a blaze.

Ten police cruisers were parked on the street, officers shielded behind the open doors with their revolvers drawn.

Hank and Bill set up a command center inside the small bakery.

The captain managed the operation from a seat at the front window, a tray of assorted donuts at his disposal.

"Make sure all the men get donuts! It's going to be a long night!" he yelled to one of the officers, who immediately instructed the young gal behind the counter to box up the confections.

Soon, every cop took a break, eating donuts and washing them down with Lovely Lotta Lattes and Dreamy Creamy Mochas, until nearly every donut was gone.

Hank approached the captain. "Folks in the back say their shift is up. They want to go home."

"Where are their replacements?" The captain wolfed down a glazed cruller.

"They're waiting outside."

"Let them in."

Bill unlocked the door.

Two swing-shift employees wearing Heavenly Donuts uniforms scurried in. They went directly to the back of the store as the dayshift workers passed them on their way out.

Bill held the door as another employee came in. He was a young kid, late teens, lean and muscular, wearing a tight-fitting T-shirt with "My Body Is My Temple" on the front and a stick-on badge with "TRAINEE" handwritten in black felt pen.

The kid seemed nervous with all the police presence.

"First day jitters, eh?" Bill asked.

"Whatever," the kid replied curtly. He strode to the rear of the store.

Bill was about to shut the door, when a young woman ran up.

"Please, I'm the night manager."

"Come on in."

"Thanks."

"I'm afraid we cleaned you out," Hank apologized, pointing to the bare shelves in the glass display case as he munched on a glazed lemon-filled donut.

"Yeah, I feel sorry for your baker and his trainee," Bill said. "They have their work cut out for them tonight."

The store manager gave the detectives a blank look. "What trainee? We don't have a trainee."

Hank wrinkled his nose. "Does anyone smell smoke?"

Acknowledgements

I would like to thank A.M. Rycroft and the Submission Team at Epic Publishing for selecting my manuscript and seeing its potential. Thanks to Deliaria Davis for showing me the economy of words and how to trim off the fat, no matter how painful. To developmental editor, Nina Johnson, thank you for your encouraging comments and reader's perspective during the editing process. Also, thank you to copy editor Daniel Santiago for his fine tuning and attention to detail. To everyone that helped get this book to press, I really appreciate your hard work.

And a special thanks to you, the reader. I hope you enjoyed *In Case of Carnage*.

About the Author

Gerry Griffiths lives in San Jose, California with his family and their four rescue dogs, plus a cat that thinks their house is a bed-and-breakfast. He is a Horror Writers Association member. He has over thirty published short stories in various anthologies and magazines, as well as a twenty-two short story collection entitled *Creatures*. He is the author of *Silurid, The Beasts on Stoneclad Mountain, Down from Beast Mountain, Terror Mountain, Cryptid Zoo, Cryptid Island, Cryptid Country, Death Crawlers, Deep in the Jungle, The Next World,* and *Battleground Earth.*

Finders Bleeders

By J. Donnait

1

He was a horror writer. I should have known. Stories of sinister psychos and paranormal entities published twice a year for the last four decades, and I thought the guy was normal. I was wrong. I found that out the hard and painful way.

It began one Sunday morning in late May while I was rummaging through a box of used books at a garage sale a couple of miles north of the Grove City Outlet Mall near Slippery Rock, Pennsylvania. It was one of the larger hunts I'd been on, and more organized, too. The house was a modest-sized bungalow that had fallen into disrepair. Dandelions over a foot tall towered over the beige lawn. The front steps had decayed, the cement crumbling into piles of rubble that sat on top of floral skeletons in thirsty dirt. The roof looked like a chessboard, missing dark-brown shingles exposing tan rotted wood. The gravel driveway stretched fifty yards in from the road. Sitting behind a table at the foot of the garage was a pudgy man wearing a white T-shirt under denim overalls.

There was a continuous cycle of cars parking on and pulling away from the berm in front of the house, which was the last thing you wanted to see when approaching a sale. For one, there was something so gratifying about shooting the shit with the proprietor of a sale full of goods and short on people. You got to learn about the person, why they were having the sale, what was valuable to them, and, if you were lucky, they'd pull something "special" out for you, for sale, but not to the general public—only to "friends." I'm sure my dad had the same feeling when it was just him and the bartender. Enter a full bar? His heart sank momentarily as he assumed that it would take forever to get his order in, or worse, that they'd be out of his poison.

At least twenty people were browsing through the clothesline with a rainbow of decades' worth of fashion, and I hated every one of them instantly. No kid likes when there are other kids hanging around an almost-busted piñata, and I saw people at sales as clueless gulls lurking for scraps. They weren't vultures, and maybe they weren't as ravenous as I was, but we were all there for the same reason: to find something we wanted. Seeing the crowd, I became increasingly paranoid, worried that anything of value was long gone, into the hands of somebody who, for whatever reason, didn't deserve it as much as I did. I rushed past the looky-loos and nearly shoved a young girl who was begging her mom to buy the plush bunny she'd found.

There were three long rows of boxes, all neatly labeled, from books and DVDs to socks and hats. Whenever there was a lot of stuff, I assumed somebody had died and it was time to get rid of the painful reminders. In a crude way, I think it was time to recoup some of that loss financially. If death turned a person's world upside down, then money helped to turn things right side up—or as right as they could be. Judging by the state of the property, though, I hoped that the proprietor might consider hiring a handyman or two.

I browsed through some of the random knickknack boxes, looking for bookends for my library shelves at home. I found none and moved on to the DVDs. *Road House*—a man's guilty pleasure and a woman's self-pleasure aid. At twenty-five cents, you couldn't go wrong. I tucked it under my arm and walked to the box of books. Whomever these books belonged to, they sure loved Evan Noble.

Not familiar with the name? He's single-handedly responsible for modern horror. He brought the genre out of the dark and made it cool. Not only can he write a million words a month, pumping out bestseller after bestseller, those books turning into Hollywood blockbusters that keep the kiddies up for weeks, but he listens to rock 'n' roll, plays guitar, and seems to know every minute detail about everything that has ever existed. The best part? He never came across as an asshole when spouting his genius. He seemed like a cool guy, talking about his main passions, passing on his sage wisdom.

There was everything in that box, from *Terry*, the story of a guy who enters puberty to discover he has the gift of mind control, to *Night Watch*, an amazing collection of short stories. I looked at the owner of the sale and wondered how nice it would be to jaw about our shared love for Noble. Being a huge fan of Noble myself, I owned almost all his stuff—everything, in fact, except for a copy of the post-apocalyptic epic *The Last*, which I'd lent to somebody and never gotten back. Remember Randy Flatts as the devil in that one? Horrifying.

I pulled *The Last* out from the bottom of the box, and before the neighboring books collapsed into the now vacant spot, I spied a small stack of paper with print on it, stapled at the corner. I exhumed the document carefully, like an archaeologist uncovering a thousand-year-old clay pot, removing the books that sat on top of it and piling them neatly on the concrete.

Taking the bound sheets out as carefully as you would bring a newborn into the world, I cradled the underside of the papers in both hands. There was a brown stain on the center of the title page, and the paper had yellowed from exposure to something—nicotine or sunlight, maybe. I didn't know exactly how old this baby was, but it felt timeworn and smelled like it had sat in a damp and dark room for too long.

It was a manuscript titled "The Murders in the Rue Morgue" by E. Noble. "**A R.I.B. Book**" was stamped in bold on the top right corner of the title page. It was about eight pages long, single-spaced, and printed on both sides of the page.

While I flipped through the manuscript, I couldn't help but feel as if I'd heard or read about this story somewhere. (I know Poe authored the original, but I mean this exact retelling.) I pushed away the inkling I had, chalking it up to nothing more than mistaken intuition. I continued to flip through it, but I couldn't ignore the whisper of a thought. I tried not to pay attention to the voice trying to validate my hunch—though it wasn't a *voice*, exactly. I'd have paid more attention to it. I'd have *heard* it. This was a prickling murmur of understanding, a thought standing last in a line of thoughts, waiting impatiently to be checked out at the register. I tucked the manuscript under my arm and continued to scan the other bins, my eyes returning to the box of Noble books.

E. Noble.

The mental lineup in my mind turned into an express checkout, and the last-in-line thought came rushing to the front.

"Jesus Christ!" I exclaimed.

Realizing that all eyes were on me, I blew out a puff of air and shook *Road House* in my hand as if it were the last copy in the world.

"This is my favorite movie, and I finally found it!" I nodded in agreement with myself and flipped the DVD around, studying the back for a synopsis I knew inside out, as if that would make me look less crazy and feel less embarrassed.

I was suddenly short of breath, my heart double-kicking. Holy shit. Holy shit. I just found a national treasure.

A couple of months earlier, I'd read Noble's *The Writ*, a memoir in which he details parts of his life, his writing habits, and his commandments for the craft. He even details being struck by a transport truck and getting hooked on painkillers as a result. Poor guy. He also talks about watching horror flicks with his friend and about how the one that had tickled him in the family spot the most was a film version of "The Murders in the Rue Morgue." He'd been so tickled, in fact, that he decided to do a novelization of the movie. He wrote and printed a whole bunch of them and sold them to his friends at school—*sold right out of them*. Talk about foreshadowing.

According to Noble, his retelling was printed on both sides of each paper, and on the top right corner of the title page, he had made sure to add his make-believe publication house in bold: **A R.I.B. Book**. *Just as Noble described it*, I thought. I was buzzing, at first from sheer excitement and then from anxiety. How did I know this was legit? How easy could it have been to replicate?

There was only one way to find out, and my appraiser would have the answer.

I rushed toward the old man sitting in a lawn chair behind a plastic folding table he'd probably borrowed from a library or some veterans' organization. A sign that read "PAY HERE—CASH ONLY!!!!" was taped to the front of what was most likely the last desk this guy hoped to ever sit behind. Judging by the excessive exclamation points on the handmade sign, I figured this guy probably got the regular, "Do you take credit cards?" In this world, people undoubtedly still asked.

I handed him the DVD, the book, and the manuscript. He squinted, adding up the cost of the movie and the book, and then something changed when he got to the manuscript. He tilted his head down and peered through the top of his specs. For a brief moment, I heard my mind mutter about how this guy knew what the manuscript was and what it was potentially worth if it was authentic. Old Man Garage Sale was going to tell me to take a hike if I didn't want to pay a small ransom for the stack of papers, trying to take advantage of someone he'd taken for a fool for enjoying a good rummage. Then I thought about how it had sat at the bottom of a box of books, and how it'd be the first thing to get soaked and destroyed in a flash flood, and how, if such a tragedy did befall such a grail in the holy world of literature, this wouldn't be the first box to be rescued. That'd be, of course, if he even gave enough of a shit to exert himself to salvage what he'd looked upon as third-rate garbage—valuable enough to sell for scraps rather than scrap altogether.

For someone who was undoubtedly in his late seventies, his forearms and biceps were thick and looked stronger than oak. He had a buzz cut and faded tattoos on both arms, proud reminders of where he'd been stationed in 'Nam, and maybe World War Two, and which battalion he'd belonged to.

"One dollar for the book, twenty-five cents for the flick, an'—" he studied the manuscript once more through his glasses, "—an' you can take the paper fuh free. That's . . ." He quickly mouthed the sum of the haul to himself. "A buck 'n' a quarter." He shot me a wink.

I gasped as if I'd been meandering through the Valley of the Shadow of "Huh?!" and someone had jumped out from behind a bush and yelled, "Boo!" I was so nervous. My ball sack shriveled up like a prune. It always happened to me before I got on a plane. *Calm down*, I told myself. *This could be a bust, is most likely a bust, so don't get your hopes up too high.*

"Thank you very much, sir," I managed to say. The pretense was crumbling, and even though I tried to be a pessimist and assume the worst, my body and mind ignored such caution and reacted as if I'd won the lottery. My heart was beating as if its time were running out, and I started to sweat. Clearly this guy had no clue what a pearl of a composition had sat in the depths of a box of his no more than a minute ago and was now conveniently in my left hand. I felt as if I were holding a bomb, felt as scared as I'd imagine I'd feel if something *were* ticking in my palm, bound to detonate at any moment. I had to say something else to this man or *I* was going to explode. Nobody wanted to do business with a crackpot, least of all a vet who was getting rid of his personal belongings.

"Nice collection you've got here," I said. "Great books. Excellent movies." I held up *Road House*, still managing to hide my giddiness and apprehension.

He scoffed. "I've never read *his* books, an' I sure as hell haven't watched *that* movie. I prefer them Harlequin Presents books n'at, especially Lynne Graham's stuff. An' if it ain't got The Duke in it, I ain't watchin' it."

Ah. A man who enjoyed the finer things. If I were to stereotype a war vet, I'd say his movie collection consisted mostly of Steve McQueen, Charles Bronson, and, of course, "The Duke". So far, we were one for one. Harlequin Presents, though? *Really?* My mom used to devour those books, and when I asked her why she liked them so much, she said it was because the people and stories were so pathetic they made her happy. Different poisons for different 'poysons,' as she used to say. My dad would say that they were for queens and grannies with dried-up cunts.

The old man continued. "This is my son's junk, anyway. That queen hasn't been back in five years an' ain't welcome back in this life n'at. I ain't gettin' any younger. At some point you gotta clean out the goddamned closet, even if that closet is a crawlspace an' it ain't your stuff."

Not knowing how to respond to such a personal confession from a total stranger, and acknowledging that the next word to come out of my mouth would be the explosion I'd been fearing, I handed him a five, turned around, and walked away, ignoring his pleas to collect the change.

I got in my car and burst out laughing. The bomb

had detonated. I wasn't within earshot of the awkward yet pleasant old man, and I had my merchandise paid for. Signed, sealed, delivered—they were mine! Thank God for small favors. Blurting out the Son of God's name on a driveway packed with people and secondhand items was one thing; acting like I was in the process of getting away with the robbery of the century, nervous and skittish, was another. Someone would have thought something was up, and I'd have dropped my wares and hightailed it out of there. Maybe the old man would have thought I was on the reefer and not taken too kindly to my type. My type *and* queens, apparently. I'd take blasphemy over botching this garage sale find of a lifetime any day.

2

I headed south on 173 toward my home in Slippery Rock. Before getting into town, I stopped at St. Thomas Cemetery to say hi to Mom. I didn't have much to say so I blew her a kiss from the driver's seat and continued on.

I sped by Buck's Bar & Grille, where families didn't go to enjoy food, where few actually watched the Pirates, Penguins, and Steelers, and where most of the down-on-their-luck and hard-up-for-cash partook in that unspoken game of How Pathetic Can Your Life Get? Home of the barfly.

I was reminded of my dad, Mr. Pathetic, brother to another Pathetic, cousin to one more still—a rotten leaf on the International Family Tree of Dipsomaniacs.

I learned that word in therapy. It's synonymous with "alcoholic," but it's more accurate; they were a bunch of fucking maniacs. They'd wince with every sip of J.D. or gag as they'd near the middle of the bottle, cringing as they swallowed what tasted like liquefied shit. There was a cowardly machismo to being a man who drank the hard stuff because it did the job, all the while wishing to Jesus in a manger that it tasted like cotton candy. They weren't much worse than the ones who did love it, and love it unconditionally and at any cost. Any cost. They who would pound the kitchen table to the beat of Blind Lemon Jefferson's "Mosquito Moan" and belt out "I love my whiskey better than some people likes to eat," as if it were the alcoholics' national anthem and they were naïve patriots.

Dad.

I hated the asshole who thought that his "friends" were the ones who sat next to him at the bar, the ol' waterin' hole, sharing in each other's miserable excuse for an existence ("Life can be so fuckin' cruel, but at least I got'chu!"), patting each other on the back and toasting to their communal complacency for a shitty life.

Dad.

Then there was the inconsiderate alcoholic. The one with a wife and children. The breadwinner. The man. He was the one who gave mom shit for not bringing enough money home ("Do they even pay you at that fuckin' job?") yet blew a small fortune on the bottle and the bar.

Dad.

The problem with living in the small town you grew up in was that you knew where the haunted houses and ghosts were, but you still stopped and stared at them, like a rubbernecker trying to catch a glimpse of a corpse in a fatal car accident. The bad memories and forgotten faces never fully faded away. They couldn't. And part of you wouldn't let them. You also couldn't leave town because that was the easy way out. You needed to stay to prove to the people dressed in their Sunday best that you had defied the odds and survived without becoming what you were raised to be.

So I stayed. My place was on 435 Slippery Rock Road. Not very imaginative to live on a road named after the small town you live in, but people don't call it the simple life for nothing. The yellow dividing line of the two-lane road had long faded to a shade of black slightly lighter than the charcoal hue of the asphalt. During the day, you could tell the difference and stay on your side, but at night, if you weren't a frequent traveler of the area? Godspeed, lad. Once every five years or so, it was likely you'd wake up to the droning sound of a car horn, and you couldn't help but fear that there was a sixteen-year-old kid with his chest pressed against the steering wheel, the pulse in the horn instead of in his heart. Sometimes, the next day, you could find shards of windshield and scraps of fender or bumper swept to the side of the road—remnants of the previous night's head-on collision. They were apt to stay there for months, constant reminders of your mortality, until the wind carried them elsewhere or they sank into the mud of a farmer's field.

That was what my neighborhood consisted of: farm fields and houses two hundred yards in from the road. Each property was about five acres. The ones that grew corn were up to fifty. On the east side of Slippery Rock Road were the barns and corn and hay fields. On the west were houses hidden behind elms that lined the road for miles at a time, standing at attention, shielding the houses from the tuneless hum of the utility poles and muffling the sound of passing cars. Private. Lonely.

Isolated.

Once south of town, and past the painful reminders, the drive home was relaxing. Nature had a calming effect, a tranquility you couldn't help but absorb. When I pulled up to my house, I put the car in park and sat idling for a few minutes, looking at the manuscript on the passenger's seat. Next to it, a cross-armed Patrick Swayze stared approvingly at me. I shut the engine off, grabbed my goods, and checked the stain of the table I'd been commissioned to refurbish. I also glanced over at my new mailbox, running my fingers over the engraved inscription RICHARD FAVREAU, which I'd just polished. Everything was drying nicely.

I opened the door to my house, a modest bungalow with two bedrooms, one bathroom, and a decent-sized kitchen and living room. The one guest who happened by whenever was my appraiser, Perry Dalton, and he always commented on the lack of family pictures. My reply was simple: my folks weren't keen on capturing moments in time. That usually made for an awkward moment of silence. My house was fairly bare, save for the bookcases in the living room, which were crammed with novels, CDs, and LPs, and the shelf in the kitchen, packed tight with cookbooks, several pages dog-eared to save my favorite recipes. I had what I needed, and anything else would have been excessive.

I took off my jacket, neatly squared away my new manuscript on the corner of the coffee table, and collapsed into the sofa with a copy of Evan Noble's latest book when the phone rang. I had a wild thought that it might be the old fart from the garage sale hollering at me that I'd ripped him off and needed to get those sheets of paper back before he had to find me and serve me up a fierce ass-kicking. An ember of panic flared in my chest.

***

If you'd like to read on, visit the Epic Publishing website for links to *Finders Bleeders* at your favorite online retailers or visit your local bookstore to ask them to order a copy for you.

Notes from the Publisher

We hoped you enjoyed reading this book as much as we did. Please help the author by leaving a review on your favorite online retailer, Goodreads, or BookBub.

Follow the Epic Publishing blog to get book news and inside information about our authors.